NO TOLLING BELL

Jon Marks

Acknowledgment:

A very special thanks to Karen Packwood, for
your help and guidance in getting this book into
print.

For  and ▮▮▮▮▮.

You know who you are.

One

A black van sped along the country lanes of South Nottinghamshire, headlights on full beam lighting up the hedgerows. Inside, a six man unit. Two up front, four in the back. The driver was an ex traffic officer of twenty years standing. The co-driver sat beside him, navigating.

The four men in the back sat in silence. Unit Leader Jim Price was the only one of the four who knew where they were heading. It was better that way, complete secrecy until it was time for the team to need to know. His earpiece crackled and the navigator said *"Eta seven minutes."* Price didn't respond. He looked at the man sitting opposite him on the other side of the van. Agent Joseph Brookes. This was their fourth assignment together and Price had always found him to be an absolute professional. A very quiet man, keeps himself to himself, speaks only when necessary. Ruthless with a weapon. This particular job should be a piece of cake with Brookes on board. The other two agents, Chapman and Roberts, were professionals as well of course. But Brookes would be the lead man when they arrived at the target, and they would take their command from him.

Agent Brookes could feel the Unit Leader looking at him but didn't make eye contact. He was staring at the floor of the van and mentally preparing himself for the task at hand. He knew the importance of the assignment, the necessity for it to go to plan and the consequences of failure. Although he didn't know any of the details surrounding the target and the threat they posed, he knew that, as ever, national security was at risk. Maybe global security. He sat up straight and pushed his back into the side of the van, using it as a rest. He swayed from side to side with the motion of the van as it careered around corners and bumped over potholes.

A full moon was rising. The night was crisp and clear. The lane meandered between the fields and farmsteads, shrouded in darkness, barely wide enough for two cars to pass.

Price's earpiece crackled again. *"Eta six minutes."* One more minute until the Unit Leader could brief the team on the assignment. Price himself had only been briefed 90 minutes previously. He had been summoned to Director Quibell's office at the National Tactical Bureau on Whitehall Place, London, at 10pm and informed of the assignment. Code One. The highest level of assignment. NTB protocol dictated that such a high-level security code should be treated with utmost secrecy. Even the unit assigned to carry out the mission wouldn't know the details until five minutes before they arrived at the target.

Agent Brookes glanced at Unit Leader Price. He could tell by his superior's body language that he was getting ready to brief the team. Price had sat up straight and stretched his back, rolled his shoulders slightly and cleared his throat a couple of times. He had positioned himself so that he could see the team clearly and made sure that they would be able to see and hear him. Just over five minutes to the target, Brookes guessed. The van was still hurtling along, maybe sixty/seventy miles per hour.

Brookes wondered what the National Tactical Bureau had in store for them. The NTB. The government agency that almost no one knew existed. The agency that doesn't officially exist at all. This innocuously named Bureau was set up in 1958 by then Home Secretary Simon Jenkins in the interest of national security.

Jenkins had been Under Secretary of State for Foreign Affairs during the outbreak and first couple of years of World War 2. He served under Winston Churchill as Minister of Education and Minister of Labour and National Service, before becoming Chancellor of the Exchequer in the latter part of 1951. It was under Harold Macmillan's leadership that in 1957 he moved to the Home Office and became Secretary of State for the Home Department. During his time in Government, and particularly during the years of the second great war and its aftermath, Jenkins had noticed the need for a greater national security. He had often talked to Churchill about the necessity for an agency to run alongside Mi5 and Mi6. The role of Mi5 is to keep the country safe from counter terrorism and espionage, and Mi6 is the foreign intelligence service involved in covert operations overseas. The role of the NTB was to cover up leaked information from *within* Mi5, Mi6 and the Ministry of Defence. For instance, if an important, highly sensitive document had somehow found its way into the public domain, the National Tactical Bureau was called into action to silence and cover up the leak. Cover it up by any means possible.

Brookes had often thought that it must have been a lot easier in the early days of the NTB. In the present day, there are far more ways for highly classified and sensitive information to be leaked and shared with the world. Laptops left in coffee shops, hackers breaking into top secret government networks, information shared online with a touch of a button. Since the beginning of the computer age, the workload of the National Tactical Bureau had increased tenfold.

Unit Leader Price glanced at his watch as the van made a sharp left. 23:31, not an ideal time for the operation. 03:00, Price thought, that was the best time for covert action. Less chance of people about. No traffic. No witnesses. Time was of the essence though, Price knew that. His earpiece crackled. *"Eta five minutes Sir."* Here we go. He retrieved a small tablet from his breast pocket and turned it on.

10

"Right, listen up. Target's name is Anna Farrow. Forty-one, five-six, dark hair, no distinguishing features."

He turned the tablet around so that the three agents could see a recent photograph of the target. Brookes, Chapman and Roberts committed the face to memory.

"Lives alone. No dependants. No family in the area. Parents both deceased. She has a brother, Ian Farrow. Lives with his family other side of the country."

Agent Chapman stared long and hard at the photograph on the screen. She looked so innocent, so... normal. What could this woman possibly be involved with?

"Earlier this evening," Price continued, "Anna Farrow received an email in error from the Ministry of Defence. The contents of that email are highly classified. So classified in fact, that even Director Quibell was not privy to the information contained within. The contents of the email though, I have been informed, are ultra-sensitive. If the details were publicly known, they could cause devastation not only to our government, but to all governments around the world."

Ultra-sensitive. *Devastation. All* governments. Brookes knew where this was heading.

"Eta four minutes," the navigator whispered.

"As far as we know, Anna Farrow has read the contents of the email, and an attachment to that email. Our tech team has confirmed that the email was opened and remained open for two minutes before they were alerted to the security breach. They have also ascertained that the attachment was also opened. They immediately remotely deleted the email from her inbox, as well as every other email for safe measure, and planted a virus in her laptop which shut it down immediately. They also remotely switched off her Wi-Fi and telephone line and deleted her mobile account. She has had no way of contacting anyone."

Agent Roberts knew the tech guys well, he'd been one of them before becoming a field agent. It was a very professional, reliable team. Their efficiency and capability were incredible. If they got a sniff of a situation in a particular area for instance, they could remotely shut down the Wi-Fi connection immediately and make it look like a fault with the internet provider. They could even cause power cuts to whole cities or just one side of a street if the situation called for it and the general public would blame their electricity supplier. It was a very slick tech operation. Roberts knew that if this Farrow woman had so much as flicked her kettle on, the tech team would have known about it.

The van took a corner a little too fast, still speeding through the night on narrow unlit country lanes, and the navigator apologised to the Unit Leader as the four men in the back were jolted from side to side. Price continued briefing the field team, unperturbed by the erratic driving.

"This is a simple operation, gentlemen. You have all been chosen for this assignment because of your individual skill sets. Brookes, you will lead. Get in, get the target, get out."

Brookes was the muscle man, the weapons expert, should the need arise. An intimidating figure. No one messes with Brookes.

"Roberts, it falls on you to get the team into the property. Farrow lives in a modest 3 bed semi on the main street in the village we are approaching. Should be a standard night latch locking system to the front door. Or similar. I don't need to remind you, keep it quiet and keep it fast."

Roberts was moved out of tech and into the field because of his physical endurance marks and his ability of being able to unlock any door in seconds during his advanced training.

Price's earpiece crackled once more. *"Eta three minutes."* He looked at the fourth team member.

"Chapman, you have been chosen because of your high graduation marks in covert ops. I realise you have limited field experience, but the nature of this assignment, the location of the target and the timing of the operation calls for the best covert agent we have. Your marks in this particular area were the highest ever seen at the Bureau. Congratulations, your field experience starts right now."

"Thank you, Sir," Chapman replied.

"Take your lead from Brookes and Roberts. Do exactly what is asked of you, no matter what that is. Understand?"

"Understood, Sir."

"I repeat, no matter what that is."

"I understand Sir." Chapman replied.

Price leant back and let out a heavy sigh. The van seemed to be slowing slightly.

Can't be much more than two minutes out, Brookes thought.

"OK," Price said, his eyes darting, trying to look at all three men simultaneously, "this is a Code One. Highest priority. By any means necessary, bring the target in."

Chapman's eyes widened. Code One. His first full field assignment was a Code One. Highest priority. Bring the target in by any means necessary. Dead or alive. In one piece or a thousand.

Two

Anna Farrow lay wide awake, paranoid, her duvet pulled up and tucked under her chin. The bedroom was dark. The only light came from her digital bedside alarm clock which emitted a faint soft green glow. 11:33 digitally displayed, then changed to 11:34. Anna had been lying there for twenty-seven minutes watching the display, seeing it change, knowing that she wouldn't be sleeping tonight. Her mind was racing, replaying the events over and over, not wanting to believe.

The day had been like any other day for Anna. Shower, breakfast, walk to work, walk home from work, microwave meal for one, check emails. *Congratulations, you have been selected…. Click here to receive your reward…. New this week from Netflix…*

Amid all of the usual dross, one email stood out. It looked official. It was addressed to an Anna Farrows, Head of the Ministry of Defence, marked top secret. The surname was off by one letter. It wasn't meant for her, but Anna's curiosity had got the better of her as it so often did, and she had read the email and its attachment. Now she wished she hadn't.

She hadn't had time to read the whole document in the attachment. The email seemed to delete itself. Then her inbox emptied and closed. Her internet lost connection, her phone line went down, her laptop shut down.

Now, lying in bed, staring at the clock, it dawned on Anna the possible consequences of her actions. It was no coincidence that her laptop had shut down and all of her communications with the outside world had failed at the same time. Maybe she had watched one too many films, but she couldn't help feeling that she was in a lot of trouble for opening that email, the contents of which were too devastating to contemplate. *Could this actually be real? Is this actually happening right now?*

Lying in bed was useless. There was no way Anna was going to sleep tonight. She told herself she might never sleep again, knowing what she had learned in the last few hours. She sat up in the darkness and felt the cold air around her naked shoulders. She reached over to the other side of the double bed where she had placed a t-shirt, in case she got cold in the night, and threw it on. Then Anna got up and put on a pair of old leggings and sat on the edge of the bed next to the window. She tousled her hair and rubbed her eyes, then tucked her hands under her thighs, palms down, to warm them up. Felt the warm carpet between her toes as she swung her legs slowly out of nervousness.

Anna leaned forward and opened the curtains a little and stared out onto Main Street at the front of the house. The moon was full and bright, and in the twilight she noticed three men walking up her driveway.

Agent Joseph Brookes led the way, Roberts on his flank and Chapman close behind. They moved slowly and silently, shadows in the darkness. They reached the target's front doorstep and Brookes stopped. He held his hand up and the other two agents froze. They stood motionless for a few seconds. Brookes looked over at the bay window to their right. Probably the living room. The curtains were closed and there was no sign of a light on beyond. He looked up at the first-floor window above, which was also in darkness. Brookes moved over to let Roberts get to work on the door lock.

Upstairs, Anna was already standing on the landing. She had quickly put on a pair of trainers that she kept under her bed, gathering dust. She hadn't been to the gym for a few months and was cursing herself for feeling so unfit. She peered over the landing balustrade down into the dark hallway below.

Chapman was holding a small torch, aimed at the door lock. Roberts was crouched in front of him. He studied the lock for a few seconds and then pulled out a selection of picks from his breast pocket. They were on a chain loop. Roberts thumbed through them and selected the right pick for the job. Brookes stood stone still and kept lookout.

Anna weighed up her options. The only way down to the ground floor was via the stairs, but the stairs led to the hallway, at the end of which was the front door. Three highly trained professionals were just beyond that door and were probably working on opening it at any second, she guessed. The stairs were a no-no. She crept along the landing and went into the bathroom, opposite the top of the staircase. Slowly and carefully she closed the door behind her and turned the lock. There was only one escape route. It was tricky, but it was the only option she had left. She would have to climb through the bathroom window and lower herself down onto the roof of the kitchen, then jump from there onto the patio area at the back of the house. Next, she would have to run across the lawn to the back of the garden and scale the fence to get into the adjoining garden. Then, somehow, she would have to get around the side of her neighbour's house, make it out onto the street and run like the wind, anywhere, and hide. And then… and then that's when the ideas dried up. But that was a long way off. Worry about that when, and if, the time comes. She opened the bathroom window and felt a rush of cold air.

The front door clicked open and Roberts returned the picks to his pocket. Brookes stepped forward and once again took the lead. Chapman followed him inside, Roberts bringing up the rear. They closed the door behind them slowly and stood for a few seconds, letting their eyes adjust to the darkness and listening for signs of movement. In front of him, Brookes saw the stairs. He peered up the stairwell and saw nothing. To their right, the door to the living room was ajar. He motioned for Roberts and Chapman to search the downstairs, and they disappeared through the door, Chapman first.

Brookes knew that at this time of night Anna Farrow was probably in bed, asleep or otherwise. He slowly climbed the stairs, walking as close to the edge of the treads as he could, there would be less chance of a creak there. Brookes guessed that the houses on the street were more than a hundred years old, and older houses come with their fair share of problems for an agent on a covert assignment. They gave positions away with their creaking and groaning. He had to be careful.

At the top of the stairs he paused for a few seconds and surveyed the first floor. His eyes had become adjusted to the darkness. In front of him was a closed door and to his right two other doors slightly ajar. Farrow lived alone, so Brookes guessed she would have the front bedroom. He made his way across the landing.

Anna slowly lowered herself down onto the kitchen roof, and she reached up to push the bathroom window shut quietly behind her. The roof sloped slightly away from the house, down towards the patio area. Her heart pounded as she sucked in the cold air, adrenaline coursing through her body, the fight or flight reflex kicking in. She carefully crept along the roof towards the edge.

Below her, Chapman checked the kitchen for any evidence of her whereabouts. He looked out of the kitchen window to the garden but couldn't see much. There was a tree line, probably about twenty metres away he figured. The trees were silhouetted against the streetlights of the road beyond, barely lit in the moonlight.

Anna's next move was the riskiest. She had to jump to the patio. No way of doing that silently. The patio consisted of dove grey limestone chippings with slabs spaced evenly as a walkway to the lawn.

Brookes checked the front bedroom. The soft green light coming from the alarm clock on the bedside table gave him the feeling that he was wearing night vision goggles. No sign of the target, but the duvet on the bed was warm and unmade. She had been there recently. Next to the alarm clock there was a mobile phone. Brookes checked it. The screen lit up, 'No Signal' displayed across the top.

Along the wall at the foot of the bed there was a chest of drawers. On it there was a television and a photo of a happy couple in a wooden frame. A holiday photo maybe, in front of some impressive building that they were visiting. He couldn't place it. Could've been anywhere, photo taken at street level. They looked like sightseers. Wasn't the target, could have been her parents. They looked fit and healthy. The photo looked aged, taken some while ago.

Brookes checked under the bed. It was dusty and messy. A few books, which she had obviously read and chucked under there when finished with. A gym kit, gathering dust. He pulled it out. Size 8. Slim, probably quite fit for her age, Brookes thought. There was a top and a pair of lycra leggings. A towel and a water bottle. No sign of a pair of trainers though.

He stood up and went to the wardrobe. Nothing out of the ordinary within. Dresses on the left, jumpers and t-shirts, jeans and leggings. Neatly arranged by category.

Brookes turned and surveyed the room. There was a slight gap in the curtains. He walked around the double bed and peered through. The windows were closed. She couldn't have got out that way, but she might have noticed the team from her window. She must be hiding somewhere.

Anna squatted at the edge of the kitchen roof and looked down. The patio area was in darkness, the full moon at the front of the house offering no light to the space at the back. She couldn't gauge how far it was, but she knew that she couldn't stay on the roof all night.

She gasped as she heard someone at the bathroom door above her, the first sound the intruders had made. They were trying the door and finding it locked from the inside. It gave away where she was, but it might have given her a vital few seconds. No time to waste.

She jumped and landed hard on her left ankle and fell onto her side, her face pressed hard against the gravel. At the same moment the bathroom door crashed open and Brookes stepped through. Chapman and Roberts heard the banging from upstairs and instinctively ran to assist.

Anna struggled to her feet and ran across the lawn to the side of the garden and threw herself behind a row of conifers. She lay there in the shadow that the moon was casting and dare not breathe. From where she was she could see the bathroom window. The light came on, and a moment later the window was thrown open, and Anna saw the huge silhouette of Joseph Brookes. He seemed to be staring out into the garden. The other two men were probably racing towards her position while he watched. The thought of being caught panicked her and she broke free from cover, ran to the back of the garden over the lawn and scrambled over the eight foot fence. She must have been seen but she carried on running anyway.

Three

Agent Brookes turned away from the window and saw Chapman and Roberts standing on the landing. He surveyed the map on the tablet he had retrieved from his breast pocket. "You two," he said calmly, "back outside. Go left up Main Street, hang a left on Church Street and left again onto Loxley Road. Wait there at the top of Loxley."

Brookes flicked a switch on his earpiece. It crackled into life. "She's gone Sir," he said as he watched the other two agents descend the stairs.

Inside the van parked four doors up on Main Street, Unit Leader Price had been waiting patiently for Brookes to report in. He wasn't expecting it to be bad news. How can she be *gone*? Brookes had never lost a target before, and this should have been such an easy pick-up. So confident was Price of the success of this particular mission, that he hadn't even considered such an initial outcome. It was supposed to have been an easy mission. The National Tactical Bureau had never lost a Code One target before.

Anna Farrow was a Code One. During his briefing with the NTB's Director Quibell, Price had been offered the whole department at his disposal. He had refused all but a team of six agents, including himself. He had felt that that was more than enough to secure the target, so sure was he of himself and his team. How can this have gone so wrong, so fast?

But there was no time for explanations. There was too much at stake. Anna Farrow had information that could cause a tidal wave of recriminations for this government. Not to mention devastation and panic on a global scale.

"Next move," Price said to Brookes.

"She must have gone out of the rear of the property. Chapman and Roberts en route to secure top of next street. Suggest you drive down Main Street, follow road to right and secure Loxley Road."

"Affirmative," Price replied. "Go." he said to the co-driver who had been in radio contact with Price the whole time. The van started up and Price held on to the sides as it accelerated down Main Street. He wondered how long it would be before Director Quibell would be in touch demanding an update. Quibell was a harsh leader, ruthless and short with all who cross his path. Just as Price answers to Quibell though, Quibell will be under pressure to answer to his superior. And the Prime Minister is not a man to take bad news well.

Loxley Road runs parallel to Main Street. The gardens on the east side of Loxley adjoin the gardens on the west side of Main, separated by the owners' fences and a tree line that runs down the centre, in between the gardens. Anna made her way down through the tree line. She knew she had to get out onto Loxley Road somehow but didn't want to go straight over from her back garden, she felt that would be the obvious way to go. So she crept her way between a few gardens until she could make out a fence further down that was maybe only four feet high.

The ground was muddy. The low branches of the trees poked and prodded her in the darkness, scratched her exposed forearms. She snagged her leggings a couple of times and stumbled on exposed roots as she snaked her way down through the trees. Behind her it was silent, but she was sure that they would be following her and felt it safer to keep moving.

Anna had been orphaned when she was still relatively young, and the conspiracy surrounding her parents' deaths haunted her. Since that terrible day, she had slowly grown more paranoid and untrusting of the world.

She felt that her paranoia, particularly for authority figures, had helped her on more than one occasion. But none more so than tonight, when she saw those three men creeping up her driveway. She instinctively knew that she was in danger as soon as she had read the highly classified government email that was not meant for her, and even more so when her laptop had crashed and her Wi-Fi had gone down soon after. The three men were there for her, surely to silence her, and just as surely are hot on her heels right now.

As she vaulted across the four-foot fence and made her way across the lawn towards the house on the other side, she heard a vehicle screech along Loxley Road in front of her. She instinctively made a sharp left and pushed herself hard against the fence along the boundary. They were second guessing her next move. Loxley Road was out, no escape route there.

Anna moved back over the small fence and back into the tree line where the shadows were darker and more plentiful. She made a right and moved between the fences, following the trees down, Main Street on her left, Loxley Road to her right. She knew that she had to get out of the area, out of the village. They were probably sending for backup, a sniffer dog team or whatever they used these days. She had to get far away, or somewhere where she could lose herself in the crowd.

The Van pulled over half-way up Loxley Road and the headlights flashed twice at the two agents standing at the top of the road. Chapman told Roberts to wait where he was and he ran down to meet the rest of the team. Roberts nodded. Although this was his first assignment, the intense training process that Chapman had been through to become a field operative for the National Tactical Bureau had made him more than capable of taking charge of a situation when it needed it. Price slid open the back of the van and jumped out and glanced at the houses to his left before turning to greet Chapman with a nod.

"Anything?" he asked in desperation.

"No Sir. No sign as yet."

"Where's Brookes?"

"On Main Street, in case she doubles back. Sir, I think we need-"

"think we need the IR Heli," Price spoke over the agent. "Already scrambled. Nearest heliport is East Mids Airport, it'll be here in six minutes." He touched his earpiece, "Brookes, report."

"On Main Street. Nothing yet."

"Stay there. We'll have eyes in the sky in five."

"Yes Sir."

Price touched his earpiece again and turned his attention back to Chapman. "Go back to Roberts. Keep alert."

"Sir," replied Chapman. He noticed something in the Unit Leader's eyes. A look that said *I've screwed this up big time.*

Should have had the IR heli in the air the whole time, Chapman thought, as he made his way back up Loxley. Sod the bloody agency budget. This was a Code One. Should have given it everything from the get-go.

The Night Owl. Risky, Anna thought as she made her way through the trees down towards the bottom of Main Street, where the road bends sharp right and runs at ninety degrees to Loxley Road, but it's worth a shot. And it's all she has, the only option left as far as she could tell. The Night Owl could take her out of the village and into the anonymity of the city.

Nottingham lies just over six miles North of the village. The local bus company runs an hourly service to and from Nottingham. The Night Owl is the last service of the evening and it leaves the village just before midnight. Anna reckoned it must be about 11:45, 11:50 at the latest. There might be just enough time to catch the Night Owl before it left for the night.

The problem was, the nearest stop was tricky to get to. As she neared the bottom of Main Street, she knew she would have to cross the road and make it to an alleyway that runs between the houses on the other side of Main, up towards the village school. There is a bus stop just left at the top of the alley, one of the last stops before leaving the village.

The tree line finished at a fence which formed the boundary between the last gardens on Main Street and Loxley Road and the back yard of the corner shop. Anna stood for a few seconds at the fence and checked behind her. Nobody was following her through the trees as far as she could tell. There was no sound coming from in front of her either.

She scaled the fence and stood in the back yard of the shop, listening for any signs of pursuers. Still nothing. She crept around the perimeter of the yard, keeping as far to the side as possible. She was cold, wearing just her t shirt and old pair of leggings against the autumnal night. A rat scurried past silently, a small scrap of food in its mouth, and disappeared through a hole in the bottom of the fence on the far side. She made her way past the bins and found a double bolted gate that led to the front of the shop. She'd felt safe in the darkness of the yard but felt a pang of anxiety as she undid the bolts and opened the gate slightly. The sound of the bolt sliding out of the counterplate resembled fingernails scraping along a blackboard. The sound carried in the night. A cold wind swept across her body as she stood in the gateway, looking for signs of movement. It was only when she moved through the gate that the security light clicked on and the burglar alarm shrilled out.

Agent Brookes was back at the target's house, looking for nothing in particular. He knew that there would be no clue to help him find Anna Farrow here. His experience also told him that she wouldn't be coming back this way. People on the run don't usually double back so quick, not while the fear is still fresh. In a few days or so, when the new reality had had time to sink in, they might try and return briefly for a few belongings. But not this soon after the chase had begun. That would be madness.

Brookes stood at the front bay window of the living room, surveying the road outside. It was well lit by the full moon and the streetlights. He knew the

IR heli would be here at any moment, and Farrow would be found shortly after.

He had left the front door ajar should he need a quick exit. Outside, the night was quiet, except for the wind rustling the fallen leaves in the front drive. And then, out of the silence, the sound of an alarm going off in the distance.

Unit Leader Price heard it too. He was still standing on Loxley Road, close to the van. He had been checking up and down the road, peering into driveways and gaps between the rows of semi-detached homes. The alarm seemed to be coming from a little way off, towards the bottom of the road.

"How long before the damn heli is here?" he barked.

Through his earpiece, the co-driver said, "Three minutes out, Sir."

"Do a circuit," Price instructed, "there's an alarm going off at the bottom of Loxley!"

"Sir."

The van started up. The driver executed a perfect three-point-turn and headed down the hill. Price ran after it and watched as the van drove to the bottom of Loxley and made the sharp left turn.

Chapman and Roberts had also heard the alarm and watched the van as it had sped off. They ran down Loxley and caught up with the Unit Leader before he had reached the bottom corner.

Anna had panicked and made a run for the alley on the other side of Main Street as soon as she'd heard the alarm, the noise and the light giving her the impetus she had needed to run for her life. She sprinted over the road and made it to the alley before Brookes had made it half-way down Main Street, and she was half-way up the alley before she turned around and saw the van pull into the shop car park, headlights on full beam. She turned and kept on running, praying she was still in time for the bus. As she sprinted towards the top of the alley the sound of the shop alarm died away and she was certain she could hear the hum of an engine growing louder from somewhere in front of her. She saw lights growing brighter at the end of the alley, and she ran as fast as she could, knowing this was her last chance to get out of the village, away from danger to the anonymous safety of the city.

Anna made it to the top of the alley and ran out into the road an instant before the bus made it to the same place. The driver slammed on her brakes and the bus slowed, but not enough to stop the inevitable collision. Anna bounced off the front of the bus and rolled down the road as the bus came to a halt.

Agent Brookes met the van in the shop car park. The alarm was loud and shrill as Brookes had a quick look around in the shop yard. He quickly ascertained that behind the shop there was a tree line between the gardens running up between Loxley and Main, leading straight to the rear of the target's garden. It must have been Farrow who had set the alarm off, no doubt about it. Where was she heading, coming this way? He retrieved his tablet and studied the map again as he made his way back to the front of the shop.

Price and the other two agents were there to meet him. Price, breathless from his sprint from Loxley to the shop, marched over to Brookes. "What the hell happened?" he bellowed, over the piercing noise of the incessant alarm.

"Farrow came through here," Brookes replied, still studying the map on the tablet screen.

"Mind telling me how she made it this far? Mind telling me why she isn't in the back of that van right now, mission accomplished?"

Brookes ignored Price's questions. Nothing to be gained from having a full blown argument about what had happened and whose fault it was. Where was she heading, where would she try and get to, where is she? That was all Brookes was concerned about right now.

Price turned his back on Brookes after getting no response. He went across to the van and spoke to the driver. "Heli?" was all he said, dejectedly.

"Any moment now Sir," the driver responded. Price looked up to the skies, maybe in an attempt to see where the damn heli was, the driver thought, or maybe to pray for some divine intervention. If the target had got away, there would be some serious questions asked about the leadership of this mission, and serious repercussions for Unit Leader Price.

This was a Code One, after all. Could be bad for all of them. Especially if the seriousness of the leaked information known by the target was leaked further.

The driver felt the phone in his pocket vibrate. He never heard it ring due to the alarm from the shop piercing the night. He answered it and listened. Turned to Price.

"Sir, it's Director Quibell. Wants an update."

Four

The driver of the bus helped Anna up the stairs and into the front seat. She was shaken, and the left side of her head was grazed but not bleeding too hard. She slumped down and took a moment.

"Are you all right, love?" the driver asked, crouching down beside her, concerned. "I… I didn't see you until it was too late. You just ran out into the road and…"

I just ran into the road, Anna thought, coming to her senses. *I just ran… I need to get out of here.* "Can we just go, please?" she shouted.

"Sorry? Go?" the driver replied.

"I haven't got any money," Anna pleaded. "But I need to get to Nottingham as soon as possible. I will pay, but I can't just now." Anna checked behind her, the bus was empty apart from the driver. She glanced over to the top of the alleyway, sure that at any moment her pursuers would emerge.

The driver climbed into the bus cab and pushed the button to close the doors. Stuck the gear stick in first. As the bus started moving she studied her passenger in the rear view mirror. Pretty, she thought. Obviously in some trouble. It was a cold night and she was wearing just a t-shirt and leggings. Came from nowhere and threw herself in front of the bus. Desperate to get to the city.

Anna could feel the driver looking at her. For some reason it unnerved her. She was grateful of course for the ride and the help. But right now, understandably, she was more paranoid and untrusting of anyone than she had ever been. She moved to a seat in the rear half in the bus.

Unit Leader Price handed the phone back to the driver. It had been a difficult phone call, to say the least. Director Quibell was not happy. Price looked over at Brookes, who was still studying the map on his tablet. Price wanted to lay all of the blame for the current situation at the agent's feet. Brookes had never let a target get away so easily, he was so professional and lethal. The best the Bureau had.

But Price knew he himself had made mistakes too. Put too much faith in his own ability and that of his team. Should have accepted more resources when Quibell had offered them.

Brookes interrupted his thoughts. "Sir!" he cried, over the alarm. He had been studying the map on the tablet.

"Brookes," he replied.

"I need the van. I believe the target is trying to get to Nottingham."

"Explain."

Explain, thought Brookes. Price wasn't on his game at the moment, that was for sure. Too worried about the recriminations should the assignment fail. "She'll be trying to get somewhere where we can't find her. Not safe in the village. Safer in the city."

"So how does she get to the city from here?" Price asked.

"The late bus. Leaves two minutes to midnight according to the timetable. If she made that bus, we need to stop it before it gets to Nottingham."

Price checked his watch. "If that bus was on time, it's only a couple of minutes away."

"I've got the route," said Brookes. "Give me the van, I can get to the bus."

The driver and navigator were already climbing out of the van before Price had agreed the new plan. Price needed to assert his authority on this mission again, he knew the team might be losing faith in his leadership. At this moment in time though he couldn't think of any better option.

"You two," he motioned to Chapman and Roberts, "search the area in case Brookes is wrong. You others, back to the target's house. Retrace Farrow's steps, be ready for further instruction." They all nodded and left.

Brookes sped off from the shop car park and along Main, past the bottom of Loxley, and headed towards the outskirts of the village, using the same route as laid out on the bus operator's website.

The alarm finally abated, the noise still ringing in the Unit Leader's ears. Price stood out on the road outside the shop and looked up and down the street. Looking for what, he didn't know. Any clue, any sign, any way out of this mess. Director Quibell needed results, he was due to meet with the Prime Minister shortly for a briefing. Whatever the outcome of this mission was now though, Price knew he would be dragged over the coals.

The sound of the helicopter broke the silence. Price looked up and saw a beam of light shining down on the other side of the village, coming his way. His earpiece crackled. "IR heli here, Sir."

"Concentrate on the gardens between Loxley and Main in the first instance, then a broader sweep of this side of the village. Looking for lone individual. Report any and all immediately."

"Will tell them, Sir."

"Chapman, Roberts you get that? Stay on this channel and await any instruction from the heli."

"Sir," they both replied in unison.

The helicopter ducked left and swung over the centre of the village towards Price. He felt a slight relief. If the heli didn't find the target, he thought, then surely Agent Brookes had jumped to the only other conclusion. Farrow would be theirs very soon.

The bus was making good progress. They were already out of the village and only a couple of miles to the main Nottingham Road. In five minutes or less they would be on the A52, the dual carriageway that runs a couple of miles west of the city. There was very little traffic at this time of night.

38

Anna sat back in her seat towards the rear of the bus, allowing her eyes to close despite her current level of paranoia. She was trying to come to terms with what was happening and needed to concentrate. The contents of the email and the attachment that she had partially read were playing over and over in her mind. Still not quite believing what she had seen. The devastating implications.

And then she thought about the huge silhouette of a man in her own bathroom just a short while ago. Looking down on her as she desperately tried to escape, her intuition and paranoia telling her to get as far away from him as she could. He and the others that she had seen creeping along her driveway, obviously there to do her harm. To quieten her, in case the secrets that she had inadvertently learned were divulged.

She thought about the route that she had taken down to the shop yard, through the tree line between the gardens. Anna looked at her arms and noticed she had been scratched a few times by the branches and bramble. She'd never felt it at the time, adrenaline had taken over her body. She'd also never noticed the cold night air. Now, sitting in the bus, she started shivering. Maybe with the cold, probably with the shock that was beginning to set in.

She thought about her brother and his family, two hundred and forty miles away. She hadn't seen them for a long time, and now she missed them. Missed her nephews' hugs and her sister-in-law's cooking. Missed her chats with her brother. Since her parents had gone, and her brother had moved away, she had felt increasingly lonely.

She thought about her parents. She missed them too. Anna was only in her early twenties when they were killed. She had become obsessed with the details of that fateful day. She pushed away anyone who tried to get close to her. Became increasingly distrustful of authority. Hid herself away from the world, except for going to work. Spent most of her time trawling through the internet, reading articles and theories on the circumstances that led to her parents' deaths.

Anna rubbed her upper forearms in a vain attempt to warm herself. The bus slowed as it came to a T junction, before pulling out and turning right onto the main Nottingham Road that led to the A52.

Agent Joseph Brookes expertly navigated the dark country lanes from the village towards Nottingham. He estimated that he would catch up to the bus in only a couple of minutes, taking into account his current speed. He surmised that the bus would have left on time, certainly no earlier than the timetable stated. It wouldn't be long before he would spot the taillights.

Brookes replayed the evenings events so far, to ensure that he had not missed any little detail. The target had escaped through the bathroom window moments after the team had arrived. She must have been awake and had the good fortune to be looking out of her window at the precise moment that the team were on the driveway. She must have been in the bathroom as the bedroom was checked. Made it to the garden as the team were upstairs. Made it to the shop yard and over the road whilst the team were elsewhere. Made it to the bus while the team were preoccupied at the shop. Might have even heard the bus and got to her quicker if not for that alarm going off.

Never mind. The heli is searching the village, and any minute now, the bus will be in view.

Brookes took his foot off the accelerator slightly and cut across the wrong side of the road as he navigated a sharp right, accelerating once more as he cleared the corner and approached an incline. The van left the road slightly on the brow of the hill. On the other side, the lane ahead stretched out in a straight line and, about half a mile ahead, the red lights on the back of a bus came into view. Brookes put his foot to the floor.

Over the sound of the revving engine, Price's voice. "Negative so far on the heli search. Sweeping the south of the village."

"Eyes on the bus. Coming up to it now," Brookes replied.

"Report immediately the moment you have her."

Will do, thought Brookes, will do. Like Price's instruction wasn't standard protocol. The man is losing it. He's messed up big tonight. Should have had the heli up from the start. Maybe more men just in case. That's probably playing on Price's mind right now. A man like Price, he'll be thinking of his own damage limitation first and foremost, the success of the mission will be a close second.

Brookes got about two hundred yards behind the bus and started flashing his main beams. The brake lights on the bus glowed for a second. Brookes slammed the van into third from fourth and floored it, still flashing the lights, and pulled out onto the opposite side of the road. The bus slowed further, down to forty mile per hour Brookes guessed.

He quickly checked the road ahead was clear, then started his overtake. It was going to be very tight along the country lane to pass the bus. He drew level with the back seat and the passenger side wing mirror clipped the bus and broke off, and Brookes swerved slightly right, the wheels almost on the grass verge on his side, kicking up dust and mud. The bus slowed further.

As Brookes got level with the centre of the bus, the van hit a pothole which knocked it left and the front of Brookes' vehicle scraped along the side of the bus for a couple of seconds before he could recover it. Sparks flew in the dark night.

The bus came to a standstill, the driver obviously realising the danger of the situation. Who was this lunatic, so desperate to get past right here? The dual carriageway is only a couple of minutes away for God's sake! The van smashed off the bus's wing mirror as it passed, then it slowed and pulled in diagonally in front of the bus. A huge figure of a man dressed in what the driver presumed looked like some kind of official military uniform got out of the van and approached the front of the bus.

Brookes rapped on the door. "Open up."

The driver hesitated, one hand over the door release button. "Who are you?"

Brookes rested his hand on his holster, gun clearly visible, and repeated himself. "Open up."

Shaken, the driver pushed the button. The door swooshed open. Brookes climbed the three steps up to the driver's cab and surveyed the inside of the bus. It looked empty. "Any passengers?" he asked, looking down the aisle.

"None right now," the driver remarked, stunned.

"This the last bus back to Nottingham?"

"Yes, this is the night owl. May I ask who you are?"

"Official business. You sure no passengers?"

"Just dropped four off in the village. Nobody gets the bus back to Nottingham on a Thursday at this time."

Brookes stared at the bus driver for a few seconds. Looked a little shaken, a little tense. Understandable given the circumstances. Could be hiding something.

"Turn the engine off."

The driver did as instructed. The engine died and there was silence. Brookes stood and listened for any movement. The driver sat still and stared at the gun on the agent's hip.

"Hand me the keys," Brookes said.

Again, the driver complied. Brookes slipped them into a pocket on his jacket sleeve. The driver was about to speak. Brookes raised his finger to his lips and gave the universal sign for shut the hell up. Stood there listening for any sound, any movement. Nothing.

Brookes moved slowly down the aisle of the bus, scanning left and right in between the seats in each row as he went. Hand poised over the gun on his hip.

About halfway down, the driver called "There really is no one except you and me here."

Brookes glanced back and gave the driver a stare, then continued his search. Slowly made his way down to the back of the bus. Empty. Thought for a second or two, then sprinted back down the aisle, down the steps and ran back to the van. The bus driver watched in disbelief as the van reversed, missing the front of the bus by a matter of inches, and sped off ahead, towards Nottingham.

Chapman and Roberts were back with their Unit Leader.

"Nothing Sir," Roberts said.

"Nothing from the heli either," Price responded.

The target was no longer in the village. Brookes must have been right. She got out on the last bus. He must have her in custody right now. Price was desperate to know what was happening but knew he would have to wait for Brookes to report in. If he tried to contact Brookes, he could compromise the agent's position if silence was of paramount importance. Fortunately he didn't have to wait long.

"Sir, Brookes. Target not secure. Not on the bus."

"Not in the village either, Brookes, so where do you suggest she disappeared to?" Price replied, almost sarcastically.

"Must have got out some other way. En route to Nottingham now. Suggest you send the heli to follow the road into Nottingham and look for vehicles speeding towards the city."

Chapman spoke to Price. "Sir, she could have got into a house and is lying low indoors. Suggest the heli checks all homes in this area for any movement inside."

"Needle in a haystack," Price responded to Chapman. "They will pick up the heat signature of everybody, anyone of which could be the target."

"But there won't be much movement," Chapman replied. "Thursday night, after midnight, most people will be asleep. Heli is here now, we are here now. If she didn't make the bus, the target could well be still here."

Price considered the options, both of which could be wild goose chases. His gut told him that the Chapman idea was the most immediate, maybe had the best chance of success. But Brookes was the more experienced agent. Chapman, a rookie on his first op. Surely the veteran would make the best call. Then again, Brookes is already on his way to the city, Price had to trust his actions. Sending the heli might be a bigger waste of time and resources. In situations like this, Price knew to always trust his gut.

"The heli is to search properties, and direct agents to any suspicious behaviour seen."

The driver and the navigator were currently searching Anna Farrow's house. The driver spoke for both of them. "We're standing by Sir."

"Brookes, continue to Nottingham. Report in at regular intervals."

"Sir."

Price watched as the IR heli swooped overhead and concentrated its cameras on the houses at the bottom of Main Street. The infrared and thermal imaging capabilities of the latest cameras weren't known to the general population. It is widely understood that these cameras can't see through walls or even windows, it is only the heat signature on the surface of buildings that can be detected, therefore using them to find people hidden inside buildings is useless. The infrared and thermal imaging cameras at the disposal of the National Tactical Bureau however, comprised of the very latest technology, modified by the geniuses that work in the tech division. Capable of picking up the heat source from a rat in a cellar.

There was nothing Price could do now but wait, again. He rubbed his eyes and cleared his throat and listened to the chuff-chuff-chuff of the helicopter blades hovering overhead. There must be something he could do, something active, something positive.

"Brookes," he said, still thinking.

"Sir."

"Where is the bus you stopped? You think maybe she could have got out somehow?"

"Almost impossible. I would have seen or heard. The bus is on the lane between the village and the Nottingham Road."

Price checked the map on his tablet. "You sure it's still there?"

"Yes Sir. I have the keys."

A wise move, thought Price. "Affirmative, I'll check it out. See if she got out. Speak to the driver."

"Sir I…"

"I have to do something!" Price interrupted. "We can't let her slip through our fingers again, can we Brookes?"

Brookes said nothing. Doing ninety on a dual carriageway is not the best time for pointless arguments.

Price beckoned Roberts over, while Chapman walked up Main Street, following the course of the helicopter. He could see curtains twitching in upstairs windows, curious residents no doubt woken by the helicopter and the shop alarm.

"Roberts," Price said, "think you can hotwire a car?"

Roberts retrieved the lock picks from his breast pocket. The nearest car was a small family hatchback on the driveway of a nearby house. "Give me thirty seconds," he replied.

Five

Anna swayed slightly in her seat as the bus she was in sped towards the city. She was grateful for the help that the kind driver had given her. Amber streetlights shone off the windows. Up ahead, traffic lights glowed red and the bus slowed to a crawl. Anna had been lost in her own world for the last few minutes, thinking about her predicament and her family.

This situation was serious. So many questions. *Who were the uniformed people that had shown up at her house a short while ago? What did they intend to do to her? Are they tracking her, are they closing in on her position right now? Is there no chance of escape?* So many questions.

And what would she do next? Couldn't go home, couldn't phone anyone.

Her intuition was telling her that she had to keep running. Those guys were the bad guys and, after what she had read on that email, she was in serious trouble. Best choice of action, get lost in the city somewhere. Get there, then think about the next move. She had to think like one of them and trust her instincts. Trust the paranoia that she believed had served her well in the past.

Anna looked out of the window and tried to get her bearings. After a few moments she realised this wasn't the usual route the bus takes into Nottingham. She moved a few seats closer to the driver.

"Erm… Excuse me, where are we?" she said.

The driver looked at Anna in her rear-view mirror. What kind of trouble is this woman in, she thought to herself. "Just coming into the city now, love."

"This isn't the usual way though, is it?" Anna asked, confusion in her tone.

"No, it's not the usual way. We had to detour."

"What for?"

The driver thought for a long moment. "Oh, just the usual. Night works on the A52. Don't worry, be there in a few minutes. How's your head now?" she asked, changing the subject.

Anna felt the graze on her forehead. Wiped it a little and felt blood on her fingertips. She recalled the moment that she had run out of the alley, straight into the path of a bus. The headlights dazzling. No time to dodge the vehicle. The shock of the impact. Seeing stars, literally. Bouncing off the front of the bus and landing on the tarmac, back first, legs flailing in the air. Lying there, staring up at the black starry sky, not quite unconscious, not quite awake.

"Sore," she said.

"Get that seen to as soon as you can love," the driver replied.

Anna wiped her hands on her leggings to get the blood off. She screwed her eyes tight shut as the first pangs of a headache started. She looked out of the windows, first left, then right, before leaning into the aisle and looking out of the windscreen. They were travelling parallel to the River Trent, along the embankment. Strange route to be taking, Anna thought. She caught the gaze of the bus driver in the mirror. Not one she had seen before. But then again, she wasn't on the night owl often. Anna then noticed for the first time that the driver wasn't wearing the usual uniform. No lanyard ID around her neck.

"This *is* the night owl, right?" she asked.

The driver said nothing, just kept on driving. Anna felt another wave of paranoia wash over her. A familiar feeling. It happened so often, she couldn't remember a time in her life when the smallest detail didn't trigger a feeling such as this. It happened so often, it almost felt comforting. It reminded her she was alive and alert.

"Sorry, but this *is* the night owl?" she repeated.

The driver glanced at her in the rear-view mirror. She could tell that her passenger was becoming restless, agitated. Couldn't have that. Needed the situation to remain calm. Easiest way to deliver her safely to her destination.

"We'll be there in a few minutes love," the driver reiterated, as soothingly as she could muster, as she was putting on a fake local accent and trying to sound like a bus driver, whatever that sounded like.

Anna didn't like the response. *Where*, exactly, is *there?* Who was this woman and why would she not answer the question. Because this was not the night owl, Anna assumed, this woman does not work for the bus company. This woman works for them. Works *with* them. She'd walked straight into their trap.

Anna replayed the evening, trying to think how they could have caught her so easily. They were the bad guys, the professionals. She was the novice, the amateur in this game. After they had shown up at her house, the only way out for her was through the back. Only one direction of escape. Across the back garden, over the fence. Of course, they should have found her sleeping in her bed and picked her up right away, but bad guy professionals like them always had to have a back-up plan. They would have known that the only way out was over the back fence. They made themselves known on Loxley Road, made enough noise to wake the dead. Didn't want her going out that way. They must have gambled that she would follow the tree line down to the shop yard at the bottom of Main Street. Easy assumption to make, as easy as assuming she would try to get out of the area. The alley off Main Street up towards the school would be the obvious choice for an escape route once the front of the shop was reached. They would be closing in on her from the left, coming down Main Street, and the right, coming down Loxley Road. Only option left was to go across the road and up the alley. Where the bus was waiting.

This bus, she now found herself trapped on. Led to the slaughter like a sacrificial lamb.

And now, as she thought back, Anna knew she should have realised that this wasn't the usual bus and driver. The bus had driven into her, yet there was no offer of first aid. The driver had carried on as normal, driven her to Nottingham as soon as Anna had asked her to. No questions asked, just started the engine and driven here. Surely normal procedure would be to care for the passenger, offer first aid?

Anna slumped back in her seat and bowed her head.

The driver had been watching Anna and could tell by her body language that she was getting more agitated with every passing minute.

"Listen love, you're safe."

"Safe?" cried Anna, "what do you mean? What's going on?"

The driver thought for a moment, then replied. "I can't say too much. You have to trust me. Where I am taking you, you have to believe, it's for the best. For your own safety, I mean."

"My safety? How much danger am I in?"

"I can't answer that. Because I don't know."

"Are you working with them?" Anna asked.

"No." answered the driver.

"Then who are you?"

The driver said nothing. Anna watched the route that they were taking. The bus drove over the Nottingham canal on Wilford Street, past the Navigation Inn on the left, down to the lights at the

53

junction at the bottom of the hill. Left hand lane of the two heading into the city, both of which bear right onto Castle Boulevard. Then immediately left onto Maid Marian Way. Up the hill, past Castle Gate and Hounds Gate, doing just twenty miles per hour now. Light traffic. The bus turned off the Way, left onto Friar Lane. Pulled up on the left. Stopped. The driver switched off the engine, opened the cab door, closed it behind her and walked back to Anna.

Unit Leader Price and Agent Roberts pulled up behind the night owl bus. Roberts tapped Price and motioned towards something ahead, out of the windscreen. The driver was leaning against the side of the bus, half-way through smoking a cigarette. They exited the hatchback and walked over, looking left and right as they went, searching and listening for any movement coming from the fields on both sides.

The driver, a portly man, balding, red faced, glanced over and sighed. Two more men in military uniforms. *What the hell is going on.* "Can I help you?" he asked, somewhat sarcastically.

Being the driver of the night owl, he had seen most things in his fifteen years of bus driving service. Drunks, fights, seats covered in vomit, young lovers engaged in the act on the back seat. He'd even been held up three times. But tonight was on another level. He'd nearly had his vehicle pushed off the road by some lunatic who had then proceeded to search his bus and steal his keys. And now here were two more jokers, obviously looking for the big hulk who was here a short while ago.

Price walked up to the driver and read his lanyard. Bob Wrightson. Photo on the ID matched the man standing in front of him.

"Mr. Wrightson," Price said, and held up his tablet, "You seen this woman tonight? Pick her up on your last trip back?"

Bob Wrightson checked the photo on the screen. Took another drag of his cigarette. "Nope. I already told your colleague, nobody on the bus. What is this about?"

"Can you tell us exactly what happened when our colleague showed up, Sir," Roberts asked.

"Your man showed up, smashed into the side of my bus. I'll be making a complaint by the way. Never had so much as a scratch on my shift before tonight. Anyway, he stops me, takes my keys off me, so I'm stranded here."

"That's it?" Roberts replied. "He took your keys and left?"

"No, he searched the bus first. Took his time too. I told him it was empty and he was wasting his time, but he searched it anyway. Then he just ran off back to his van, sped off down there…" He pointed along the straight lane.

Price had been listening whilst looking out into the blackness over the fields, looking for any movement. The moon was full but offered little light to help.

"Thank you for your time, Mr. Wrightson. Apologies for your bus."

Price turned to Roberts. "Double check the bus again, just to set my mind at ease. We can't leave any stone unturned here. I'll get the heli over here, do a sweep of the fields just in case."

"Sir," Roberts said and went around to the door of the bus.

"Is that it?" Bob Wrightson said, "What about me? I'm bloody stranded here."

"I understand your concern Mr. Wrightson. Unfortunately we have a situation here that is more pressing. Please go and wait further instruction inside your bus."

"My concern? I'm pissing fuming! Who are you?"

Price took two steps closer to the bus driver and grabbed him by the throat in one swift movement. Pushed his Adams apple back with his thumb and held it there for a few seconds. Bob Wrightson struggled for breath, then went limp. Price released his grip and dropped the driver to the floor. Not dead, just unconscious. Price didn't need a disgruntled loudmouth as a distraction.

The driver sat on the seat in front of Anna. Anna looked up, fear and confusion in her tear-filled eyes.

"Who are you, and what is going on?" Anna whispered.

"You're safe. You must trust me. My name is Terri. That is all you need to know about me. I'm just the courier."

The courier, Anna thought, and what am I, just a package?

Terri continued. She'd dropped the fake accent. "I don't know anything about you, except that you are in danger. I was told to be at a certain place at a certain time, and to bring you here. To explain to you what you must do next if you want to stay safe..."

"Wait," Anna interjected, "You were told to pick me up from near the top of that alleyway?"

"Correct."

"But who told you? How did they know where I would be? That doesn't make sense."

"You will find out who. As for the how... I can't answer that, as I don't know. Please let me continue. Now, as I was explaining, I was instructed to bring you here. Do you know where we are?"

"Near the castle." Anna pointed out of the front of the bus. She knew the area, and the history behind it, very well. Ahead, the road curved slightly. Just beyond the curve there was one of the visitor entrances to Nottingham Castle, the Main Gatehouse. Around the corner to the left, the world-famous statue of Robin Hood stands, bow and arrow in hand. The statue was commissioned to mark the visit to the city by the Duke of Edinburgh and the Princess Elizabeth in 1949.

Cast in bronze and weighing half a tonne, the seven-foot statue stands on a block of Clipsham stone and aims the tip of his arrow at the gatehouse of the castle, the scene of the final battle between Robin and the Sheriff of Nottingham, so legend decrees. Nearby there are statues of Little John, Friar Tuck and other members of his 'merry men'. Robin stands outside of the castle wall behind, representing the outlaw as an outsider to the establishment. The castle wall looms large behind the statue, with 4 plaques embedded depicting the various legends. The battle with Guy of Gisborne's men. The fight between Robin and Little John at the river. The marriage of Robin to Marian. A dying Robin shooting an arrow in the air to mark his final resting place.

Anna's favourite pub was just down the hill beyond the statues. Ye Olde Trip to Jerusalem. The Trip, as it's locally known. Reportedly the oldest inn in England, legend has it that Richard the Lionheart gathered his men here before travelling to Jerusalem and the Crusades. The pub is built into the Castle Rock, the giant promontory rising 40 metres on which the castle itself stands.

"Correct," Terri said. "The castle is straight up. My instructions are to bring you here and give you instruction of how to get inside the castle walls. Inside, you'll be safe."

"Inside the castle?" Anna was more confused than ever. She wasn't sure whether she should trust this Terri. The whole night had been too crazy, and now this. Fleeing from home, literally running for her life. Knocked down by a bus. Kidnapped by a mysterious woman. And now storming a castle. "Why do I need to get inside the castle? And how exactly?" As an habitual paranoid, she knew not to trust anyone, least of all mysterious kidnappers. And yet, this woman had got her to Nottingham, helped her to get where she wanted to go, where she thought she would feel safer.

"As I said, inside the castle you'll be taken to safety. You have to get out of the area, they are coming for you and they are ruthless. They will not give up until your silence is guaranteed. Believe me when I say that they have eyes almost everywhere. The safest way out of Nottingham for you is beyond those castle walls."

Anna threw the courier a confused glance.

Terri continued. "Getting into the castle is easier than you would expect. If you walk up to the castle and bear left along the castle wall, you will pass the statue of Robin Hood. Follow the wall boundary. There are various doors of different sizes set into the wall. Pass the Friar Tuck statue, you will be descending a hill…"

Down towards the Trip, Anna noted, where the pedestrianised area turns into Castle Road. She pictured the area in her mind. She'd been there a hundred times or more.

"A little further down, the stone built wall of the castle is replaced by the natural castle rock. The castle is built on this rock as you must know. There is an information board set on a stand. Pass the board and there are three doors set into the castle rock. The third door you come to from this point will be unlocked. This will lead to the network of caves and tunnels that exist within the rock and beneath the castle."

Terri stood up and moved back to the driver's cab. Retrieved a torch and tested it a couple of times. Flicked it on and off. It was an extremely bright beam, Anna noticed. It would need to be, to help her see once inside the tunnels. Terri walked back to Anna and handed it to her.

"It'll be dark in there, but this will help. Once inside the door, move forward along the tunnel, then you'll turn first left, then second right. Go straight from there. You'll come to another door that opens out into a courtyard. Cross the courtyard into the gardens. There you'll be met."

"Why all the secrecy?"

"I would have thought that was obvious. You're in grave danger. I don't know why, I'm not told this. My best assumption would be that you know something of great interest to my employer, something that you are not supposed to know. Something that the men who were after you would rather you were dead. I am here to instruct you on how to get to safety."

Anna weighed up her options. She could just run once she was around the corner, hide someplace. Away from whoever was chasing her. Away from whoever this Terri character was working for. But something bothered her. Why had someone gone to all this trouble of helping her. How did they, whoever *they* were, even know she needed help. How did *they* know where she was going to be when the bus they had sent picked her up. Too many questions, too little answers. And she needed answers.

Six

"You have to go now," Terri said, "Good luck. Here, take this." She handed Anna her jacket. Anna put it on. Dark Blue fleece. It felt warm from the heat of Terri's body. It smelt faintly of perfume. It made her feel safer somehow.

Anna looked down at the torch she was holding, then up into Terri's eyes. Terri nodded slightly and offered the faintest of smiles. The contents of the email flashed into Anna's mind again. Terri had made the correct assumption. The information contained in the email would have devastating consequences should it be leaked. This country would never be the same again. That's why she had to be silenced.

As she descended the bus steps and the door closed behind her, she thought again of just running. Down past the castle, back to Castle Boulevard then up to the railway station. Can't be more than a five-minute sprint. Jump on the first train to anywhere. Seemed a good option. But Anna knew she would never get any answers as to what was happening to her if she took that option. She decided to walk towards the castle anyway, both options required that at least. Gives her more time to think.

The bus started up and moved away from the kerb. Anna turned and saw Terri wave at her. She put on a false smile and nodded in reply. Anna watched as the bus disappeared. She zipped up the fleece and turned up the collar. The night was getting colder. She stuffed the torch into the fleece pocket and walked up Friar Lane towards Nottingham castle. There was no one around.

Anna walked up to the castle and stood there for a few seconds looking at the twin-towered gatehouse. The sight sent a shiver down her spine, the prick of a sharp memory. Her heart grew heavy. She shrugged the feeling off. Then she made the left, onto the wide pedestrianised walkway that snakes down the hill past the Robin Hood statue. To her left were a couple of bars, closed for the night. On her right, the area around the statues were lawned, and Anna crossed the grass and walked close to the castle wall, away from the streetlights. She glanced over at the statues. Being there brought back better memories. Childhood memories. Having her photo taken with her mother, sitting on the grass. Her father, pretending to run away from the arrow pointed straight at him. The guided tours of the Nottingham caves and tunnel network with her brother.

There would be no tour tonight. Anna shook the memories out of her head and concentrated on the instructions she was given. Third door past the information board. Once inside, first left, then second right, then straight ahead to the courtyard.

Anna followed the castle wall down to a set of steps which took her around one of the round towers set into the wall. She followed a small path, the decline becoming gradually steeper. In the wall she noticed a small wooden door, gothic in style, arched and pointed at the top. A door into the tunnels. Then she passed another, same style. Then a third. But she hadn't made it to the information board yet, this wasn't the right door. Anna went down some more steps, which took her back onto the main pathway. In front of her was the information board. The cobbled pedestrianised area turned back into road at this point. She looked right and left, up and down the hill. Nobody in sight. She breathed heavy and followed the path down. Her trainers were rubbing on her bare feet, she felt her heels stinging. Her ankle was throbbing from where she had landed hard on it earlier. She crossed the road to survey the area, to get a broader view of the castle rock and the doors therein. From the opposite side, she could just make out the Trip, just around a corner, set into the castle rock. There were three doors in front of her, all in the same gothic style. She studied the three doors. The first two were bolted and secured with a padlock. The third door was just bolted. There were four steps leading up to it. Anna noticed that the castle wall above the door had been worn away over the centuries, exposing the Triassic sandstone rock behind.

Another wave of paranoia consumed Anna. This was it. Decision time. Run away to the railway station, board a train and get far, far away. Or trust the courier Terri and follow the tunnels to safety. *The safest way out of Nottingham for you is beyond those castle walls.* She felt the weight of doubt. Instinct and curiosity told her to take the tunnel. Panic and fear told her to take the train.

She needed more time to decide. Anna walked further down the hill and sat on a bench, head spinning. She sat there for a few moments, staring down the hill. At the bottom, maybe a hundred and fifty yards away, Castle Boulevard ran at right angles to the road she was on. Very light traffic. A police car screamed past, blue lights flashing. A taxi went by in the opposite direction.

And then Anna saw someone walk around the corner, coming off Castle Boulevard and up the hill towards her. She squinted, and her heart missed a beat. She recognised the huge silhouette instantly. He must be about six-three, six-four, she supposed. Athletic build. Broad. Strong physique. Walking with purpose.

The last time she had seen him, he had been standing in her bathroom window, backlit. An image she would never forget. She froze for a second, then her fight or flight response kicked in.

She fled up the hill. Back to the third door. She vaulted up the four steps and tried the bolt on the door. It was rusted and old and moved only a couple of millimetres on her first attempt. Anna glanced back down the hill and saw the huge silhouette advancing on her position. She turned back to the bolt and wiggled it as hard as she could. The bolt slid back slowly, a little more with each pull. The silhouette came closer, a hundred yards away now.

The bolt squeaked and moved slowly. She tried harder, moving the handle on the bolt up and down as she pulled back. It moved slightly.

Eighty yards away, the silhouette advanced. The bolt squeaked louder and louder with each turn and pull. Moved slightly with each twist. Desperation written all over her face, Anna tried even harder. Twist and pull. The bolt moved slightly.

The silhouette was sixty yards away. An arm bent, a hand raised up to the hip. Walking with purpose. Anna put one hand on the stone door archway for leverage and with her other hand she twisted and pulled the bolt handle as hard as she could. It barely moved.

Forty yards away, the silhouette drew a gun and held it in two hands in front of his massive bulk. Anna pulled and pulled, twisted and twisted. The bolt squeaked but stayed put. In desperation, Anna hammered on the door. Tried to shoulder barge it open.

She turned to look at the silhouette, twenty yards away and closing.

She realised there was no time to loosen the bolt. No time to run away. He was ten yards away. Anna put her back against the door and slid down it. Put her hands inside her fleece pockets, defeated. Put her head on her knees and shivered. Waited.

The huge silhouette lowered his gun. Didn't need that now. He stood silent in front of her and re-holstered his weapon.

Anna looked up at him. Strong face, huge neck. Broadest shoulders she had ever seen. Some kind of earpiece stuck to the side of his chiselled face. Military style uniform, covered in pockets. Triangular body shape, thick legs. His eyes were cold and dark, as far as she could tell in the relative darkness. Shaved head. Short beard and moustache, dark but greying. Anna noticed a scar on his right cheek.

"Get up," he ordered.

She shivered again and considered her options. Get up and die. Stay down and die.

"Get up!" he shouted. Anna flinched and stood up. Slid back up the door using her knees, keeping her hands in her pockets. Kept her head down. He moved a couple of steps back and touched a button on his earpiece. Said something. Anna couldn't make it out, her mind was elsewhere. Racing at a million miles an hour. Her feet were stinging, ankle throbbing, head pounding. She surmised he was calling in with the good news. Target acquired. Secret's safe, never to be told.

And then, in a final attempt to escape, a plan came to her. A desperate, foolish plan. Desperate people resort to desperate measures. It couldn't get any worse, even if it failed. And fail it surely would, but Anna would never forgive herself if she didn't at least try.

Agent Joseph Brookes turned his back on Anna Farrow momentarily to finish his conversation. When it was over, he flicked the button on his earpiece and looked up and down the hill. There was nobody around. Checked his watch. 00:40. Friday morning. The city sleeps. He turned back to where the target was standing and was blinded by a strong beam of light. His pupils constricted instantly, the pupillary response reflex protecting the rest of the eye from the intensity of the light. Then the light disappeared and he was momentarily blinded. Brookes felt something hard crash into his chest. He stumbled backwards and lost his footing on the four steps that led up to the door. Fell backwards and smacked his head on the hard concrete of the path below.

Anna stood with the torch in her hand. She put it back into her pocket and instinctively went back to work on the door bolt. The Agent was prone on the floor, coming to his senses. With a few more twists and pulls and squeaks, the bolt freed itself and Anna threw the door open, entered the tunnels and slammed the door behind her.

Agent Brookes lay on the floor and watched the door slam shut. He rubbed the back of his head and checked it wasn't bleeding. Then stood up and dusted himself down. Took a moment. Straightened his jacket. Checked nothing had fallen from his pockets. Walked up the steps. Checked up and down the hill. Nobody around. He threw the bolt back over the door and locked Anna Farrow inside. Only one way out now. She was trapped, right where he wanted her.

Seven

Brookes double checked the door was secure. It was. He turned and walked back down the steps, then left up the hill towards the pedestrian area where the statues are. As he walked, he surveyed the buildings on the right, opposite the castle. Checked every building meticulously. No sign of life. As he drew level with the statues, he crossed over to the castle side of the broad walkway over the cobbles. Checked the castle walls, checked the streetlights. Further up, he studied the imposing twin-towered gateway to the castle. Then crossed back and turned the right corner into Friar Lane. Made his way down to near where the bus had stopped a short while ago. A faint smell of diesel still hung in the air. Checked the buildings on the left and right side of the street. All was good. No CCTV on any building between the tunnel door and the spot he was now. Perfect. He pushed the button on his earpiece.

"Sir," Brookes said.

"Brookes. Where the hell… Where are you?" Unit Leader Price responded immediately.

"In the city. Nottingham railway station, Carrington Street. Outside. She could be trying to catch a train."

"That another hunch?" Price said, half-heartedly.

"Any luck in the village?" Brookes responded, sarcastically.

Price had no answer. The heli had drawn a blank. A couple of possibles, turned out to be dead ends. A couple having a row in one house, a man getting ready for a night shift in the other. Nothing in the fields near where the night owl bus was stranded either.

"Sir, I think it's worth checking out. It's what I'd do, if I was trying to get as far away as possible."

"Agreed, worth checking out. Report back anything and everything."

"Affirmative," Brookes said. He heard Price ordering Roberts to get the tech guys to check out the CCTV in the station area, then switched the button on the earpiece to off. Took it out of his ear. Dropped it to the ground and stamped on it with his size twelve regulation issue boots. Picked up the pieces and dropped them in a nearby bin attached to a lamppost. Walked back towards the castle.

Unit Leader Price and Agent Roberts were back at the village with Agent Chapman, the driver and the navigator. Price and Roberts had driven back from the stranded bus and returned the stolen hatchback to the driveway that they had borrowed it

72

from and walked up Main Street to meet the other three at the target's house. The helicopter had been dismissed; it was useless now. If the target had reached the city, tracking her down with the heli would be impossible.

The phone in the driver's pocket started ringing and vibrating. Price held his hand out and took the phone and moved into the kitchen at the back of the house. Closed the door behind him.

"Sir."

"Price, report." The stern, cold voice of Director Quibell.

Price gazed out of the kitchen window and thought carefully about his reply. In the moonlight, he could just make out the outline of the garden, through which the target had escaped.

"She's in the city, Sir. We believe she's in the area of Nottingham Station. Agent Brookes is there now."

Silence on the line for a second, before the Director replied. "You've lost her. That's what you are reporting Price. You've lost her. Do I need to remind you of the consequences of this?"

"No Sir," Price snapped back. "Our top agent is there now. If she's there, he'll find her. Tech guys are checking CCTV in the area also. She can't have gone far." Try and end the conversation on a positive, Price thought.

Director Quibell didn't even respond to Price's last remark. He ended the call and slipped the phone back into his trouser pocket. Shifted uncomfortably in the leather chair he was seated on, one of twenty-four around the vast table in front of him. He had made the short journey from his own office at the National Tactical Bureau to 70, Whitehall, London, after his previous conversation with Price. On arrival, he had been chaperoned straight into the main Cabinet Office, briefing room A, or COBRA as it is known.

Director Quibell placed his hands flat on the highly polished table-top, beads of sweat on his bald head glistening in the light from the chandelier. The room was warm. Very warm. Quibell always felt uncomfortable in COBRA. Whenever he had been summoned there, it was always for an important briefing, usually for when things weren't going to plan.

Opposite, sitting across the table in a decidedly more comfortable looking leather chair, the Prime Minister.

"Well?"

"Sir, at approximately eleven thirty-five this evening, a six man team arrived at the house of Anna Farrow…"

"I'm well aware of the facts so far, Quibell!" the Prime Minister boomed, hands clenched into fists on the table. He was wearing a t-shirt, hoodie and jeans, the first time Quibell had seen the leader without a suit on. Must have got dressed quickly. Some minion had woken him to give him the bad news. His hair was dishevelled. He had obviously been filled in with the events so far and had been rushed to the Cabinet Office for emergency talks.

"She's in Nottingham, Sir!" Quibell snapped back, the pressure he was under building. He caught himself, calmed himself, and continued. "She's in Nottingham, Sir. Agent Brookes is checking out the most probable area as we speak. The tech guys are scouring the CCTV."

The Prime Minister looked at Quibell sternly. The Director was sweating. He had beady eyes set too close together and a long, thin pointy nose. His suit looked cheap, the sleeves were slightly too long and the buttons were plastic.

It was no secret that the two men didn't get along. A clash of personalities. They were too alike. The PM admired the work of the National Tactical Bureau and understood the need for someone like Quibell at the helm, but that didn't mean they had to get along.

"We *will* find her, Sir," Quibell said.

"*We* had better," The Prime Minister replied.

The tunnels under Nottingham Castle were colder than the outside air. Anna had made her way down the sandstone steps that led to the main tunnel. It was dark and damp. This part of the tunnel and cave network were not on any of the guided tours. The tunnel was lower and narrower, the ground uneven, not suitable for the general public in these days of health and safety. The only light came from the torch that Anna had used as a makeshift weapon a few moments ago.

First left, then second right. That was Anna's mantra. First left, then second right. That was the way to the courtyard, across which lay the castle gardens. The path to safety. As she made her way along the claustrophobic passageway she wondered who would be meeting her. Anna's choices had been made for her. She knew her only option now was to trust Terri and do as she had been instructed. No chance of reaching the station and boarding a train now.

The tunnel was long and straight and seemed to be narrowing even further. The air was cold and dank, and tasted funny with every breath she took. Anna flicked her torch from left to right, illuminating the smooth sandstone walls. She was grateful for the fleece she'd taken from Terri. Up ahead, the torch light caught the entrance to another tunnel going off to the left. Her stomach knotted. As she neared the entrance to the left tunnel, she heard a bang from a long way behind. A door slamming. The sound reverberating down along the straight tunnel. The silhouette was coming for her. She ducked left and picked up the pace.

Agent Brookes stood inside the door and let his eyes adjust to the new darkness. He retrieved a small torch from one of his many jacket pockets and flicked it on. He descended the steps and stood crouched over at the end of the tunnel. His broad shoulders almost touched both sides of the small passageway. Brookes shone the torch along the tunnel, the light fading before it had even reached halfway down. He made his way down the tunnel with a quick shuffle. Bent over to avoid cracking his head on the tunnel roof. He turned his body sideways as the tunnel narrowed, to get his shoulders through. He held the small torch in his right hand and with his left he felt along the wall, pushing himself along. His boots were scuffing across the floor, the sound echoing, no time for covert action now.

Anna hurried along the new passage. She steadied herself on the uneven ground by keeping to the right and feeling along the wall. A fast walk, not quite a jog. The tunnel had widened slightly but seemed even lower than the previous one. She crouched slightly. Her heels were burning, probably bleeding she guessed. Adrenaline pushed the pain to the back of her mind.

The wall to her right gave way. The first tunnel on the right. *Second right* she repeated to herself. She paused for a second and listened for any sound behind her. Nothing. She could hide here down the first right tunnel. Stay stone still for a while so he couldn't hear her. He would never find her in the labyrinth carved into the Castle Rock. Anna turned off the torch and waited. The absolute blackness and all-consuming silence unnerved her. She felt disorientated for a few seconds. Then, from in the distance, she could make out the shuffling of large feet. Growing louder as it neared her position.

Agent Brookes shuffled along the long straight tunnel, which seemed to be closing in on him with every step. He wondered what this particular passageway had been used for in centuries past. Probably smuggling people in or out of the Castle. An escape route maybe, for if the castle was stormed and the nobility residing there needed a quick getaway.

Up ahead, his torch beam exposed another tunnel running off to the left. He stopped at the intersection and took out his phone. The screen lit up and he squinted slightly. Pushed an app icon marked 'track' and after a few seconds a map appeared. Not much information on the map, the area of the Nottingham Castle nothing more than a green blob. He used his thumb and index finger to enlarge the map, filling the screen with the castle grounds. Towards the bottom-right corner of the area, a blue dot flashed slowly. Brookes' position, far beneath the castle. The tunnels and caves not marked. He zoomed in further, concentrating on the south-east portion of the map. To the west, and slightly north of his position, a red dot flashed slowly. The target's position. The red dot wasn't moving.

Brookes took the left tunnel, the quickest way to the target by his reckoning.

Anna daren't move as the sound of the footsteps had stopped behind her. Now she could hear them again, and they seemed to be coming down the passageway she found herself in. She turned the torch on and came out of the first-right tunnel. She glanced left and heard the footsteps a little clearer. There was no light. Anna turned right and continued along the low passageway as fast as she could in the cramped conditions. The air grew colder and damper the deeper she got into the underground maze. It was more unpleasant to breathe, and she felt the urge to cough with every inhalation. She ducked further as the tunnel became lower. Her hair brushed the roof. She imagined the tightness of the tunnels would work in her favour. She was five-six, her pursuer a good ten inches taller. He would struggle a lot more than her.

Anna wondered what lay ahead, what answers she would get as to what was happening, who these people were that were trying to help her.

She could still hear the shuffling footsteps behind, but they didn't seem to be getting closer. Ahead, she could just make out the entrance to the second-right tunnel in the distance. She would soon be out into fresh air again. She prayed that the doorway to the courtyard was easier to open than the last door had been.

Anna made the second-right tunnel and turned into it. She noticed that the floor was sloping upwards, a gradual ascent. She continued along the new passageway, hoping this one was shorter than the others. The tunnel widened and the roof raised.

Agent Brookes arrived at the first-right tunnel. He paused and studied the image on his phone. The blue dot had moved slightly towards the centre of the screen. The red dot ahead, north-west of his position, moving slowly as it flashed. He was headed in the right direction. He shone his torch down the passage on the right. Nothing. He continued straight. His shoulders had a little more room to move along this tunnel, but the roof was getting lower, making speed an issue. It was an awkward shuffle, stooped over. It would be far easier for a shorter, leaner person. He picked up the pace as much as he was able to.

The tunnel Anna was in opened out into a small cave area. Straight ahead, the tunnel continued. She shone the torch around. Almost circular, she guessed the cave was about twelve feet across. The air was particularly dank in this area. It smelled fusty. She turned the torch off, looking for any signs of natural light. There were none. Pitch black. She turned the torch on again. Studied the outer walls of the cave. Set at intervals of around six feet, there were recesses that stretched floor to ceiling. Deep enough to hide a person, should the need arise.

Behind her, the footsteps echoed along the chambers. The silhouette seemed to know where she was going. She suddenly had options again.

Continue on to the courtyard and trust Terri. Hide in a recess and hope the silhouette passes her by, then double back and escape somehow.

Trust Terri. That's all she could do when there was only one option open to her. Now, as ever, Anna's paranoia kicked in once more. Should she trust this stranger? She had done her no harm, and actually helped her out when she had needed it, but trust her?

As the footsteps grew louder, Anna ducked into one recess on the left side of the cave and turned off the torch. She fitted inside comfortably. The utter darkness of the cavern felt good.

Agent Brookes arrived at the second-right tunnel. Stopped and surveyed the map again. The blue dot near the centre of the map, the red dot closer and directly north. Not moving. Brookes noticed the tunnel was wider and the roof was higher, which came as a relief. He was still very fit and strong, but the peak of his performance abilities were a year or so behind him. The tunnel was taking a toll on his back and being able to stand straight a little more would ease the pressure off the lower muscles. He took the right turn. He shone his torch along the passageway ahead and noticed the floor going uphill slightly. The way out. It seemed to be another straight tunnel. The red dot was motionless ahead. The blue dot flashed slowly and drew even closer to it. Why was the target stationary? She had found a hiding place.

Brookes slowed to a crawl, even though he was able to stand straight and walk normally. Ahead, he noticed that both sides of the tunnel disappeared. Must be opening out into a bigger chamber. As he moved, the red dot changed its position from due north to north-west. The blue dot very close now. He memorised how far it was to the mouth of the opening, then turned off his torch and moved slowly towards it, treading very carefully. He returned his phone to his pocket and walked along in the blackness.

Anna stood stock-still in the recess. The sound of the footsteps had ceased, which sent a small ripple of panic through her body. She stiffened, tensed. Perfect silence and sheer darkness. Her breathing was short, shallow. She tried to slow it down. She could hear her heart pumping. She pushed herself back into the recess as far as she could. Just ahead of her and slightly to the right, Anna could make out an occasional crunch of boot on sandstone.

Brookes entered the small cave. He could sense the space around him. He paused and listened. Turned to his left, towards the area where he believed the target was hiding. In the blackness in front of him, he could make out the faintest of breathing. He inched closer and gauged she was only about two feet in front of him. A faint smell of perfume rose out of the dankness. He stepped silently towards her. The closer he was, the less chance she had of making a run for it. Another step forward, then he whispered softly. The words came out of the darkness like a crash of thunder, accentuated by the utter silence that surrounded them.

"*Don't move.*"

Anna froze, scared rigid like a rabbit in the headlights. She knew it was over. She was defeated. Terri's voice resounded in her ears. "*You're in grave danger,*" she had said. "*The men who were after you would rather you were dead,*" she had also said.

The whisper came out of the dark again. "*Don't move.*"

Brookes turned his torch on and shone it into the recess. Anna Farrow threw her arm over her eyes and turned away. He looked at her. Didn't look much like the photo Unit Leader Price had showed the team in the back of the van less than eighty minutes ago. Hardly surprising, after what she'd been through tonight. Her dark hair was messy and bloodstained. Her clothes were dusty and dirty. She was shivering.

"Turn around," he ordered. "Put these on." He handed her the handcuffs that were clipped to his waist.

Anna turned around as he shone the torch to the ground. He could sense fear behind her eyes. She looked at the cuffs and then up at his face. He wasn't smiling. The torch threw a shadow over the left side of his face. The scar on his right cheek looked more prominent, emphasised by the harsh light. She took the handcuffs and clipped one loop over her right wrist loosely. Brookes quickly tightened it, not so much that it would hurt, but tight enough so that she wouldn't try and break free. He clipped the other cuff around his left wrist. No chance of escape now.

Eight

The National Tactical Bureau cannot be found on any map. Type it into Google and nothing will show up. Of the thirty million visitors that travel to London every year, not one of them has the NTB building marked on their itinerary.

Director Quibell made his way back to the Bureau along Whitehall after leaving COBRA. He'd been driven to the Cabinet Office in a car sent by the Prime Minister. On the return trip, Quibell declined the offer of a lift. Walking helped him think, and he needed to clear his head. Ridiculous to drive anyway, Quibell thought. It was barely a five-minute walk back to the Bureau. For the Prime Minister, it would take much less than that to get back to 10 Downing Street, which joins onto the Cabinet Office building at the rear of both properties. They are joined via another building which overlooks the gardens of Number 10 and the parade ground at Horse Guards. He doesn't even need to go outside, hence his scruffy appearance a few moments ago. Just a few long stuffy corridors to walk down and the PM would practically be back in bed.

Quibell exited the Cabinet Office building and turned his jacket collar to the wind. Wished he'd brought his hat with him. He looked to his right down Whitehall and could see the railings that keep Downing Street secure. Further down, the Cenotaph, and in the distance, the imposing square Victoria Tower at the Palace of Westminster.

Quibell turned left and walked north along Whitehall. He passed the Women of World War Two statue, behind which stood the Ministry of Defence building. Quibell gave the MoD building a derisory look as he passed and wondered what was happening behind those walls at this moment in time. This mess was all their fault. Over half of all the work carried out by the NTB involved covering up for their mistakes. And this one, by all accounts, was the mother of all cock-ups.

Further on, he glanced at the bronze statue of Field Marshall Earl Haig, Commander-in Chief of the British Forces on the Western Front during World War One, sitting astride a powerful charger. Next, Quibell passed the Duke of Devonshire statue opposite the entrance to Horse Guards and the Household Cavalry museum. Then he walked past another equestrian memorial, this one of Prince George, the Duke of Cambridge. In front of him, at the top of Whitehall, Nelson's column towered into the London skyline, fifty-two metres high.

Quibell drew level with Admiralty House, then crossed the road and walked into Whitehall Place. He walked past the Old War Office building, with its four distinctive domes, the site of Winston Churchill's War Office during World War Two. Eleven hundred rooms spread over seven floors. It was dissolved in 1964, when the Ministry of Defence took over its operations.

Just past the War Office, Quibell paused and looked behind. Whitehall Place was quiet. There was nobody following him. There never was, but it didn't stop him checking and reassuring himself every time he drew level with the office. He slipped a key card into a narrow slot hidden in the wall under a post box. A camera mounted high up, level with the fourth storey, swivelled in his direction and stayed pointing at him. He gave an impatient wave at the lens. A couple of seconds later the door adjacent clicked open, an armed guard waiting for him.

Agent Brookes walked in silence along the final tunnel, Anna Farrow by his side, head down. Up ahead, his torch shone on the gothic door to the courtyard. Brookes looked at Anna, then back to the door. The tunnel was wide enough here for them to walk side by side. He still had to crouch a little in places. The air quality improved.

They stopped at the door. Brookes shone the torch around and found a latch. The door swung outwards into the courtyard beyond. Anna hesitated as Brookes walked forwards. He sensed her tense up.

87

"Come on," he said, looking down at her. "Not far now."

"What are you doing?", she replied. "Who are you? What is happening to me?"

Brookes hesitated, standing just beyond the door. Anna stood in the doorway, framed by the gothic architecture.

Brookes spoke calmly. "My name is Joseph Brookes. I… work for a government agency that deals with threats to national security. What you know is seen as a threat to that security. You have been classified as a Code One. Highest threat level. I was sent to ensure that the threat was eliminated."

Anna thought for a second. Her eyes widened as she heard those words. "You were sent to kill me."

"If that was the best outcome for the country. Yes."

"So where are you taking me? Why not kill me here?"

"You'll find out," Brookes replied. "Right now, you have to come with me."

Brookes started walking across the courtyard, Anna following, being half dragged, her right arm raised out in front of her attached to the Agents' left wrist. The gravel crunched beneath their feet. The cold air felt clean and fresh as she breathed it in.

In the distance, across the courtyard and somewhere out towards the lawned gardens of Nottingham Castle, Brookes could hear the low hum of a helicopter.

Director Quibell entered the tech office and surveyed the bank of screens on the back wall. The lighting was subdued, soft. Half a dozen men and women were milling about, talking on comms, studying monitors, zooming in on areas, zooming out.

Kelvin White spotted the Director walking over to him, pulled up an empty chair to his desk and paused the image on the screen in front of him. Kelvin was the best tech guy in the National Tactical Bureau. Due to his size and his love of fast food, he knew he could never be transferred to the field ops as Roberts had been. He didn't have the physical attributes of his former colleague.

"Got anything, White?" Quibell shouted, in the manner Kelvin was accustomed to from his superior, as he sat down in the empty chair.

Kelvin pushed the enter button on his keyboard. The image on screen showed an empty street. "This is footage from the CCTV camera mounted on the front of Nottingham railway station, looking left down Carrington Street." A taxi appeared and stopped at a set of traffic lights. Behind, the white headlights of a speeding vehicle approached. The speeder shot through the red light and disappeared off screen to the right. Kelvin rewound the tape slightly and pressed the pause button when the vehicle was in the centre of the screen. The time stamp in the bottom-left corner of the screen showed 00:32.

"That's our van. Agent Brookes, arriving at the station, driving past the main entrance at the front," Kelvin explained to Quibell. The Director nodded.

Kelvin minimised the paused image and brought up another window. "This is from the CCTV mounted on the side of the station, on Station Street."

The new video played. Station Street runs at a right angle off Carrington Street down by the side entrance to the station. It was pedestrianised but plenty wide enough for vehicles. From the bottom-left, the speeding van entered the screen and flew down the street, exiting the camera's field of view top-right. Kelvin let the video play on. Nothing happened.

"OK," Quibell said, "so we know Brookes was at the station. That ties in with the intel. Anything else?"

"Nothing, Sir. I've surveyed the CCTV footage from the cameras along Carrington Street and Station Street. No sign of the target or Brookes entering the railway station. No sign of them leaving the area. No sign of either of them at all, as it happens. Could be that they entered the station as the cameras were pointing the other way, they rotate at forty second intervals, there or thereabouts."

Quibell stared at the screen, deep in thought. "Anything else from other areas?"

"Working on it now Sir. Checked thirty in the city centre so far. Nothing out of the ordinary."

"Send a van for the team. We need to get them to Nottingham."

"Already on its way Sir. Ten minutes away. We had a team on a Code Three in Leicester."

"Good. In the meantime, keep checking those cameras. Any word from Brookes?"

"No Sir. Maintaining radio silence at present."

"Let me know when he makes contact. I'd like to hear what he has to say for himself."

Kelvin nodded, as Quibell got up and left for his office.

The harsh gravel of the courtyard gave way to damp grass at its boundary. The sound coming from a helicopter grew louder. Anna looked up to the skies, then back at Brookes, who seemed unperturbed by the noise. They made their way across the garden area of the castle grounds. The noise seemed to be coming from an area behind the high cherry laurel hedge at the far end of the gardens.

Brookes knew what was waiting for them. She would be OK. Safe. For him though, hard times ahead. He knew he would be half dead in a short while. Beaten to within an inch of his life. Willingly. Had to be done, he realised that.

Anna interrupted his thoughts. "How did you find me?" she asked.

"That fleece you're wearing," he offered as a reply.

Anna wasn't satisfied with the answer. "How did you know I was at the castle?"

"That fleece you're wearing," Brookes repeated, "it's chipped. A tracking device."

Anna walked on behind the agent, who had slowed his pace so she could keep up more comfortably. The courier, Terri, had given her the fleece to keep warm, or so she had thought. Now it seemed there was an ulterior motive. It was also so that Brookes could track and find her. Capture her. *Brookes was working with the courier.* But that didn't make sense to Anna. Brookes works for a government agency that kills people like her, civilians who have found out too much. The courier on the other hand, had helped her escape the village. Told her how to get through the tunnels to where they are now, because she would be safe if she came this way. So then why is Brookes bringing her this way? *Brookes is working with the courier.* None of it added up.

Brookes could sense that Farrow was disturbed and confused by the answer. He noticed a bench about twenty yards to their left, away from where they were headed. He changed direction and made for the bench. Anna had no choice but to follow.

"Sit down," He said.

Anna sat. Brookes followed. He turned the torch off. They could barely see each other in the moonlight.

"Listen to what I am about to tell you and try and take it all in," the agent whispered, quickly.

Anna shivered, wrapped the fleece around her as tight as she could, and nodded back at him.

"The government agency I work for is called the National Tactical Bureau. As I have said, we deal

92

with threats to national security. Specifically, leaked information from inside our own government. We try and protect this country from the morons who work *for* this country, if you like. If some highly sensitive top-secret information gets into the public domain, we shut it down."

"Are you going to shut me down?" Anna whispered back.

"No. There are… let's just say there are people higher up than the National Tactical Bureau. I also work for them." Brookes squinted at Anna. Tried to gauge her reaction. She looked back at him, confusion written across her face.

"Other people? Who are these other people?"

"That's them," Brookes motioned with a nod of his head in the direction of the cherry laurel hedge. "That's their helicopter you can hear. They are going to take you away from here. You will be safe with them."

"But who are they?" Anna asked.

"They'll tell you. And you'll trust them. They can protect you."

"Why should I trust them? Why should I trust you? You were sent to kill me, after all."

Brookes looked at Anna's face. Her expression was one of dejectedness, but there was still a spark of fire behind her eyes.

"Earlier tonight, *they* learned of what had happened. How you had come into possession of a highly classified, top-secret email. How you were made a Code One. How the National Tactical

Bureau were brought in to silence you. I was contacted by *them*," he motioned towards the hedge again, "and ordered to get you out to safety. Code One's don't happen often. Rarely, in fact. The NTB assigned me to the case, and these people contacted me shortly after."

"So, what, you're a double agent or something?"

"If that's how you want to think of it. Yes. I had to be seen to be doing the best job I could do for the NTB, and at the same time, I had to protect you and bring you here to safety."

Anna leant back on the cold bench and tried to process the information she was receiving. She still looked like she would need a lot more convincing if she was to go willingly. Brookes knew time was of the essence. He assumed he was already being missed. Questions would be asked as to his whereabouts. That's why what would happen to him shortly had to go ahead. As soon as possible. He didn't want to blow his cover.

Brookes continued. "When the team arrived at your house tonight, I knew I would need to buy you some time to get you out of there. I sent the other two agents to check the downstairs, knowing you would probably be upstairs at that time of night. I heard you in the bathroom. Could see the door was locked. Guessed you would be jumping out onto the kitchen roof. It was your only way out."

Anna looked dumbfounded.

"We have the plans for your house," Brookes said, noticing the look of confusion on her face. "We know all of the possible routes you could have taken to get out of there. The only escape route you had was through the back garden. I gave you a few moments in the bathroom and went to check your bedroom. Made as much noise as I could kicking down the bathroom door, knowing the other two agents would come rushing. Covering any sound you made getting to the ground. I watched as you ran across the garden and made your way over the rear fence, to the tree line."

Anna thought back to that moment. The huge silhouette in her bathroom window, peering down at her. She had wanted to escape out onto Loxley Road but had heard a vehicle.

"I needed to get you to that passage, to where the bus was waiting. I sent the other two agents up the street, and the rest of the team over to the Loxley Road. The only way you could go was down towards the shop. Then I gambled that you were smart enough to escape up the passage, to try and make the last bus and get to the city, knowing your pursuers were closing in from either side. It was your only option really."

Brookes hoped that by explaining his actions, he would gain a little of Farrow's trust. Make her see that he was on her side.

Anna thought long and hard. It all seemed to make sense. Typical of how the night was going though, as soon as one thing was explained, another thing took its place. *Who were these people now trying to help her, and why?*

Brookes stood up and motioned for Anna to do the same. Switched on his torch. "Come on," he said. "Let's go."

Nine

Kelvin White unwrapped his second Big Mac of the evening and shoved it into his mouth. A colleague had just returned from the 24-hour McDonalds on Whitehall, just past Great Scotland Yard. It was situated opposite the Government office of the Department for International Development. Kelvin had often mused that here, on Whitehall of all places, amongst the highest offices in the land, and surrounded by the greatest military monuments in the world, there was still room for a McDonalds. And he was thankful for that. He felt lucky to have his favourite restaurant right on the doorstep of his place of business.

There had been no sign of Agent Brookes. Kelvin had checked every CCTV in the area. Mapped them all prudently. No sign of the target either. He had studied the maps of Nottingham city centre and began widening his search.

His phone rang. A familiar voice on the other end.

"Kelvin, big man! How's it going? Roberts."

"Andy Roberts!" Kelvin replied, spitting gherkin over his keyboard, "How are you? How's life in the field?"

"Better than sitting next to you all day, that's for sure."

"Piss off. Heard you lot cocked up big time tonight, now I'm having to cover your arses. What happened?"

"Not sure. Nothing we did wrong. Maybe Price was a bit too blasé about the assignment, should've got more tech help from the start, who knows. Listen, reason I'm ringing, Price says there's a van on its way for us? Any idea when? He's going loopy here."

"Should be about five minutes out. Tell him to calm down, man of his age." They both laughed.

"I will, and I'll tell him you told him that. Got any intel for us?"

"Not much, sorry," Kelvin replied. "We've got Brookes and the van at Nottingham railway station a while ago. Caught him on two cameras, one on Carrington Street at the front of the station, the second on Station Street to the side. No sign of him entering the station. Or the target either. Checked all over, they don't show up on any camera in the area. Possible that Brookes entered the station as the camera was rotated the other way."

"So, the best guess is that they are in the station somewhere, or she caught a train maybe?" Roberts asked.

"That would have been my original thought Andy, yes."

"Agent Roberts to you, big boy."

"Ooh, listen to him. Mr. Agent Roberts. *The names Roberts. Andrew Roberts. Licensed to pick locks.* Anyway, like I said, that would have seemed the most likely place to find them."

"I sense a but coming. And knowing you, it's a pretty big butt!"

"Enough, OK," Kelvin grinned. He always took his former colleague's fat-shaming banter with good humour. He was used to it, but he knew that Roberts' heart was in the right place. "There is a but coming. For starters, the trains departing from Nottingham are very sporadic at this time of night. No trains have arrived or departed in the last hour or so."

Roberts scratched the back of his head as he listened. "Go on," he said.

Kelvin continued. "I've mapped all of the CCTV camera locations in the area of the city around the station. There seems to be an area that is not covered by the cameras. I'll patch the map with the camera locations through to Price's tablet, have a look for yourself, you'll see what I mean."

"Good work, mate. We'll take a look. And you've not heard from Brookes at all?"

"Nope, nothing. He doesn't speak much at the best of times. Could be he's maintaining radio silence because he's tracking her. Soon as I hear anything or find any other clues, I'll be in touch."

"Thanks Kelvin. Speak soon." Roberts hung up.

Kelvin took another bite of his Big Mac and patched the map through to Unit Leader Price. Sat back in his chair and looked at the burger in his hand. Shrugged, and took another bite.

Agent Brookes and Anna Farrow reached the hedge line and passed through to the other side via an archway cut out through the hedge. Standing in the middle of the large lawn was the helicopter, unlike any that Anna had seen before. The main propeller was rotating and cutting through the air loudly. Brookes flashed his torch at the helicopter and three men disembarked. Two men came out first. Anna noticed that they were of a similar height and body size to Brookes but dressed in casual clothes. Jeans and a plain hoodie. Different colours. Behind them, a much smaller man, not as tall as the other two, thinner. He was immaculately dressed from what Anna could gauge in the darkness.

Brookes and Anna waited by the archway in the hedge and the three men came to meet them. Brookes pulled a key out of one of his hip pockets and turned to face Anna. She looked up at him as he unlocked the cuff on her wrist, then unlocked his own. "No more running," he said. She nodded in reply.

The two casual looking big men joined them first. Both of them acknowledged Brookes. He looked at their faces, then nodded to each of them. The smaller man then joined.

"Good evening, good evening," he said, quite chirpily and with perfect pronunciation. There was an awkward silence as the man looked at Anna, then turned his attention to Brookes.

Anna's first impression had been correct. He wore a beautifully fitted suit. Could be black, could be dark navy. Matching waistcoat. Crisp white shirt, perfectly pressed collar. Gold tie with gold tiepin. Pocket watch chain hanging over his stomach. His cufflinks shone in the moonlight. He looked, she guessed, late fifties, early sixties. Grey hair, short at the back and sides, parted and flicked left to right. Clean shaven. He knew how to look after himself. Either that, or he had servants to look after him.

The smart man turned back to Anna. "Miss Farrow. Sincerest apologies for what you have endured this evening. Through no fault of your own, you find yourself in the gravest of dangers." When he spoke, his voice gave an air of sincerity and grandeur. "I would like to assure you, right now, that your well-being is our priority at this moment. How are you feeling?"

"Tired," Anna whispered. Absolutely shattered if truth be known.

"Of course. It is late, and you have been…"

"Confused," Anna interjected, a little more loudly. "Hungry. Paranoid. Heads banging. Feet are killing. Cold. No, freezing…"

"Miss Farrow,…"

"No!" she shouted. "I am physically and mentally burnt out. Tell me what the hell going on."

The smart man raised his hand in a kind of surrender gesture. "I understand," he said calmly. "Miss Farrow, I completely understand. Once inside our transportation, you will be offered food and drink. We have a medic on board, he will tend to any physical injuries you have sustained. We will make you as comfortable as possible. And I assure you, I will answer all of the questions you undoubtedly have, as far as I am able. Please. We are here for you now."

Anna took a couple of deep breaths.

The smart man turned to the two casual men. "All ready, gentlemen?" They both nodded. "Agent Brookes?"

Brookes nodded. He looked down at Anna and gave her a small smile. "Take care, Miss Farrow," he said. "Hope to see you again one day."

The smart man reached out and put his hand on Brookes' arm. "You know, Agent Brookes, that if there was any other alternative, I would not hesitate…"

"I know," said Brookes. "It has to be this way. And time is running out for us, Sir. We need to do this right now. It won't be long before the NTB figure out the CCTV configuration and come searching in this area."

"You're a brave man, Agent Brookes. I wish you well. A speedy recovery. I will be in contact as soon as is possible."

Brookes looked at the smart man, then Anna, before turning and walking back through the archway in the hedge. The two casual men followed silently behind, quickly disappearing into the darkness.

"What… wait!" Anna called to Brookes. He didn't reply. She turned back to the smart man, a puzzled expression on her face. "He's not coming with us?"

"Alas, no," the smart man replied. "Agent Brookes has other commitments. Unfortunately, the Bureau he works for leave no stone unturned. To ensure your safety, along with his own, he has to go back."

"What will happen to him?"

"Come. There is much to explain." He put one arm around her and motioned towards the helicopter with the other. They started walking.

"What did you mean by wishing him a speedy recovery. Is he sick?" Anna asked.

"Sick, no. Agent Brookes will have to explain his radio silence to his superiors. There will also be a huge question mark as to how a civilian such as yourself managed to evade Agent Brookes, fondly regarded as the best of the best at the Bureau. The most feasible explanation would be that Agent Brookes was unable somehow to give chase. Those two scruffy agents who left with him have the unenviable task of making it appear that Brookes was attacked." The smart man noticed that Anna looked concerned. "I'm afraid that the agent will suffer horrific injuries in an attempt to make the attack appear as realistic as possible and shield Brookes from all doubts that the Bureau may have surrounding his actions tonight."

"There must be some other way?"

"Believe me, we've gone through all the alternatives. It's not something we do lightly, Miss Farrow. Brookes has to be made to look as though he was incapacitated. A man of his size, well it takes a lot of beating to bring him down. It must look realistic. As he recovers, he'll be asked a great deal of questions about this evening. The more realistic the attack, the greater the damage inflicted on Agent Brookes, the better for him, in a perverse sort of way. Any questions he faces that he feels might incriminate himself, he can plead he doesn't remember. Amnesia, something like that."

As they neared the helicopter, Anna remarked, "I bet Brookes wasn't too keen on that plan."

"On the contrary, Miss Farrow," said the smart man, "It was his own idea."

Ten

Unit Leader Price sat in the back of the new van, Agent Roberts to his left, Agent Chapman opposite. Once again, they were speeding along the country lanes of South Nottinghamshire. Price checked his watch. 01:14.

"How long?" he barked at the driver.

The driver replied, "Twelve minutes to the station, Sir."

"Make it ten."

"Going as fast as I can, Sir."

Price was holding his tablet out in front of him. He brought up the map of the CCTV cameras that Kelvin White had pinged over a few minutes ago. Showed it to Roberts. "What do you think?" he asked.

"Two options, Sir, like the tech guys said. Brookes either went inside the station and were missed by the CCTV, or for some reason he went this other way…" he pointed to the area on the map that had no cameras marked, "and is in that area somewhere."

Price studied the map on the screen. Carrington Street ran past the railway station towards the city centre, down to Castle Boulevard. There were CCTV cameras marked at the junction, mounted on the businesses on the corners either side. That route was therefore not feasible, the tech guys would have spotted Brookes no problem. Station Street was also discounted. Further along from where Brookes must have abandoned the original van, more cameras mounted high.

"Sir, may I?" Roberts said. Price handed him the tablet. "Look here. He could have gone down this way."

On the opposite side of the road from the railway station, further down towards the city, there was a walkway just before a bridge over the Nottingham canal. The walkway descends from road level, down to the canal and run parallel to it. There was a CCTV camera pointed at the path about half-way down, but it was possible to climb over the small wall on the right-hand side near the top, and not be seen. It was quite a drop to the canal path at the bottom, but possible to lower oneself down and stay out of the sight of the camera. Once on the canal path, it was easy to stay hidden. A couple of hundred yards down there was a footbridge over the canal, for walkers heading into the city.

Roberts traced the route with his index finger to show Price where Brookes could have gone.

"Why would he go that way, Roberts?"

"Unsure, Sir. But that's the only other way he could have gone. I have complete confidence in the tech guys. If Brookes had gone any other way, he would have been spotted. Now, if he had gone over the footbridge and up through these buildings here-" Roberts pointed again at the map, to the area on the other side of the canal. The buildings on this side were predominantly canal side bars. There were a couple of walkways that led out on to Canal Street, by Castle Boulevard. The area to the north of the Boulevard was the castle district. "-he could be around this area here."

Price looked at the map. "When we get to the station, I'll take Chapman and we'll check it out. Roberts, you check out the second option."

"Sir," they both said in unison.

The smart man waved at the two-man crew sitting in the cockpit of the helicopter. The door behind the cockpit opened and the smart man stood aside and beckoned Anna in before him. She hesitated for a second, then climbed on board. He followed her. Another man was inside who closed the door behind them.

The main propeller on top of the helicopter sped up. Anna could hear the change in propeller speed, but, surprisingly, it wasn't too loud in the cabin. She had always thought that passengers would need noise cancelling headsets whilst in a helicopter, not so the case in this one. The seats were plush, very comfortable, like sitting in the back of a limousine.

The smart man noticed Anna's expression, the curiosity of her surroundings. "Welcome to the Eurocopter X3," he said. "The fastest helicopter in the world. Top speed of over 290 miles per hour. We'll be cruising at about 270 tonight."

A voice came through the speaker at the front of the cabin. "Please buckle up now. We'll be taking off momentarily." The passengers found their seatbelts and clicked them over their waists.

As well as the main five bladed propeller, the X3 is fitted with additional tractor rotors, mounted on short wings either side of the helicopter. These started spinning and the cabin shook for a couple of seconds. There were two small windows, one on either side, but they had been blacked out. No-one could see in or out.

Anna felt a sensation of weightlessness in her stomach as the helicopter left the ground. It swayed in the air for a second, before climbing vertically at a rate of twenty metres per second. She clung on to the arms of her seat and dug her nails in.

"Please try to relax Miss Farrow, the feeling will pass once we start to move," the smart man said, then paused as dizziness washed over him. He shook his head and waited for the moment to pass. The front of the helicopter, which resembled the face of a bottle nosed dolphin, dipped and then the helicopter swung high in a wide swoop, gaining speed fast.

"Hmmm. That's the worst part over with Miss Farrow. I'll never get used to it, I must confess. Frightful business," the smart man continued.

108

"Now, for the introductions." He pointed to the man who had let them into the cabin. "This is Doctor Singh. He'll take a look at that ghastly wound on your forehead."

Anna looked across at the man sitting opposite. Handsome. Well groomed. Remarkably sharp beard, but a kind face. "Good evening, Miss Farrow. Once we get to cruising height and level out, will you allow me to dress that for you?" He had a calm demeanour, befitting his profession.

Anna nodded.

The smart man continued. "Good. That's good. Please, help yourself to bottled water and snacks which you'll find in the compartment underneath your seat. Now, my name is George Butler. I'm sure you must have a thousand questions for me." Butler pushed a button on his chair arm. "How long?"

A voice over the speaker replied, "Twenty minutes, Sir."

"Thank you. Excellent. Plenty of time for a chat."

Agent Brookes was back in the tunnels under the castle, navigating along the same passageways that he had come earlier. He'd memorised the route. The two casually dressed men followed closely behind. Brookes hadn't asked their names, and didn't want to know, it wasn't important. He would only know them as the Blue hoodie and the Grey hoodie. Sounded like a couple of superheroes. The only thing that mattered to Brookes was that they were capable of doing a good job on him, without actually going too far. He had to be nearly dead for his alibi to be convincing. But he didn't want to end up really dead. The two men charged with the task of making the attack appear realistic certainly looked like they could do the job.

"SAS?" he asked, to either one of them.

Blue Hoodie was immediately behind Brookes, and he spoke first. "Yes Sir. 'C' Squadron, Bramley Camp."

"Sir. 'A' Squadron, Hereford, Sir," Grey Hoodie responded.

Brookes knew the answer already, he was just making small talk. He could tell by the way they carried themselves. He could spot a fellow fan dancer a mile off. The fact that they were wearing blue and grey hoodies, the colours of the SAS parachute wings, was merely a coincidence.

They were in the part of the tunnel where the roof was low and the walls were narrow, along the long straight section that leads to the door near the statues. They were all shuffling awkwardly, their bodies twisted, their backs slouched over.

"Medical training?" Brookes asked. It would put him a little more at ease to know that at least they would know where the major arteries and organs are. What to avoid.

Blue Hoodie again spoke first. "RAMC, Sir, before getting the call to Wales. Stationed in Nigeria."

The Royal Army Medical Corps. Finest medics in the world, according to Brookes. Precision surgery while the bombs are dropping. The Corps had saved his life before. Brookes felt a little more at ease.

"You got the call from the regiment? *They* called you?" asked Brookes as they shuffled along.

"Yes Sir," replied Blue. "Not many of us around Sir."

Brookes half-nodded. "Not many at all." Up until that moment, Brookes thought that he had been the only one.

The Special Air Service normally takes applications to join their squadrons from personnel in the Airborne and Commando Forces. Very rarely, they are recommended personnel and follow that recommendation up.

"What about you back there? Grey Hoodie. You had any medical training?"

"Not much Sir," Grey replied. "Just the basics in Belize."

"Perfect," Brookes muttered under his breath. "Can I make a suggestion, gentlemen?"

"Sir," replied Blue.

"Blue here, he does all the precision work. Grey, you just kick the shit out of me, but only where Blue says it's safe to."

"We won't kill you Sir," Blue responded.

"No, you won't," Brookes replied. "Or I will haunt your nightmares for the rest of your miserable lives."

111

Doctor Singh and George Butler had swapped seats. The Doctor was now sitting next to Anna, Butler opposite. The Eurocopter had levelled out and was cruising at 270 miles per hour. The seatbelts were off. Anna was swigging a bottle of mineral water and eating a biscuit. The Doctor was cleaning the graze on her forehead.

Anna was doing the maths in her head. 270 miles per hour. 20 minutes to the destination. That's 80-90 miles from Nottingham in 20 minutes. That's a long way as the crow flies. Due East, Anna thought, over the North Sea. West, somewhere over Wales. South, London area. North, somewhere between York and Newcastle. Basically, anywhere in the country.

The Doctor applied the dressing. He had already given Anna some paracetamol for her headache. She had studied the tablets carefully before taking them, an action that hadn't gone unnoticed by Butler. Still some work to do on the trust front.

"Let me tell you about our mutual friend, Agent Joseph Brookes," Butler said, smiling.

"Why would I need to know about him?", Anna replied.

"Because, Miss Farrow, he is risking his life to save yours," Butler remarked, quite sternly. "Now. Joseph Brookes. An army man. He was in the First Armoured Infantry Brigade. Served tours in Sierra Leone and Kosovo."

"How did he wind up working for you, whoever you are?" Anna asked, impatiently. She was fidgety, nervous still. Understandable, Butler thought.

"Please allow me to explain, if you will. There is a chain of events that led Agent Brookes to his current position. It may help you understand and answer some of your questions, if you bear with me."

Anna shifted back in her seat and took another swig of water. Replaced the cap on the bottle and said "OK."

"Good. Now, Brookes was, and is in fact, an excellent soldier. Absolutely top-notch infantryman. It wasn't long before he came to the attention of the DSF. Forgive me, Miss Farrow, that stands for Director Special Forces. The chap in charge of the UK's special forces. SAS, Marines, that sort of thing. Brookes was given the honour of being invited to train for the Special Air Service. Five gruelling weeks in the Brecon Beacons. Flew through the personal fitness test of course. Tell me, are you familiar with the fan dance?"

Anna looked confused. Pulled a face.

"No. Why should you be? The fan dance is an endurance test that the SAS candidates must face and complete against the clock. A hike up the Pen y Fan, the highest peak in South Wales, with full equipment on, followed immediately by a descent down Jacob's Ladder, then a four mile run, finishing with a two mile swim. Brookes holds the record for the fastest ever fan dance, Miss Farrow."

Anna didn't look impressed. She moved her feet and winced as she caught her swollen ankle with her other foot. The doctor, noticing, said "Would you like me to take a look at that?" Anna nodded and undid her laces. She carefully slipped the trainers off. The insides were blood stained. Her heels red raw. Her ankle was badly swollen. Doctor Singh opened the compartment under his seat and retrieved some bandages and an ice pack. He knelt down on the floor and started to gently clean the wounds.

"Anyway," Butler continued, "blah blah blah, passed his training. Earned his beret, joined 'the regiment'. Went to Afghanistan. Redeployed to Libya, where his unit helped in the fall of Tripoli. Redeployed again to Northern Iraq, in the fight against Islamic State. Exemplary record, Miss Farrow. Truly incredible what this soldier has achieved."

"This is all very interesting Mr. Butler, but what has all this got to do with what has happened tonight?" Anna asked.

"Nothing at all, so far, I agree. But hopefully it will help you understand the kind of man Agent Brookes is. Trustworthy. Reliable. A good man."

Anna nodded. Then winced again, as Doctor Singh applied the ice pack to her ankle. "Sorry," the doctor said.

George Butler continued. "Now, the SAS, as you must surely know, is the elite of the British Army. Where does one go from there. Where is the next rung on the ladder, so to speak. With such a record of great service behind him, he now came to the attention of the Joint Intelligence Committee. They initially wanted Brookes for a role within Mi6, but it was thought that a man of his superiority and mindset would be perfectly suited to the most secretive of Government agencies."

"The National Tactical Bureau," Anna said.

"Correct. The National Tactical Bureau. It takes a rare, special kind of mindset to carry out the assignments of the NTB. Highly sensitive assignments. The kind of tasks that wouldn't sit well with most people."

"Like killing innocent civilians who had done no wrong. Brookes told me all about it."

"Rarely, but... yes, should the government deem the leaked information stay classified by any means possible. I am told you are a Code One. What you have learned this evening must be ultra-sensitive."

"I can't believe it can be true," Anna said.

"And yet it is, Miss Farrow. Whatever it is. You must inform us of your knowledge once we have arrived. Of course, I'll see to it that you are given time to freshen up."

"Where are we going, can you tell me that?"

"You'll see for yourself in a little over... twelve minutes."

Twelve more minutes. They had already travelled nearly half the distance. Maybe forty miles. Anna found it incredible. It felt as though they were hardly moving.

"So you see, Miss Farrow," Butler went on, "Brookes went from infantryman to SAS, from SAS to Government Agency."

"So he's reached the top. Listen, I'm grateful to him, of course I am, for what he's done… doing for me…"

"The story doesn't quite end there though, Miss Farrow. Working for the Government. That's not *'the top'* as you put it. There is a higher office."

"What do you mean?" she quizzed.

"I mean the Special Air Service poached Brookes from the regular Army. The Government poached him from the Special Air Service. And we have poached him from the Government. He still works for the National Tactical Bureau of course, we need a man on the inside there, for such an occasion as we find ourselves in at the present moment. And we are grateful that Brookes is that man."

Brookes leaned against the statue of Robin Hood, outside the castle wall. Blue and Grey either side of him.

"Are you ready?", Brookes asked.

"Are you?", Grey replied.

Before Brookes could reply, Grey swung his huge right fist into Brookes' gut. Brookes hardly flinched. Grey opened his fingers and flexed them.

"Sorry," Brookes said. "I tensed. Force of habit, natural reaction." Grey looked at Blue. Blue looked at Grey. They both looked at Brookes.

116

"Wait a minute. Need to empty my pockets." Brookes took his phone out, gave it to Blue. Then his tablet. Then his gun, knife and his government ID. Unzipped his jacket. He was wearing just a vest underneath. "Let me relax, untense. Then try that again."

Brookes to a deep breath, inhaled and exhaled hard. Repeated. On his third inhalation, Grey swung his fist again, hitting Brookes just below his ribcage, forcing the breath out of his body. Brookes doubled over as Grey brought his knee up fast and smacked Brookes under his chin. His head snapped back awkwardly, and he fell forward on to his knees.

Blue took the knife that he'd been handed and stabbed the Agent in his thigh. Brookes cried out in pain. Grey silenced him with a quick left and right jab to the mouth. Brookes bit his cheek and felt the warm coppery taste of blood on his tongue. Blue twisted the knife and Brookes spat the blood out, his teeth stained red. Grey grabbed Brookes' collar and lifted him to his feet. A river of blood flowed down his leg. He punched him hard in the chest four times in quick succession, and Brookes felt two of his ribs crack and break. His eyes were blurred and he was fighting for breath. He tried to block out the pain in his leg. Resisted the temptation to fight back. Suppressed any feelings of panic. Grey smacked him square on the mouth again, cutting his top lip open and dislodging a tooth.

Blue kicked the back of his legs from under him. Brookes collapsed onto the statue of Robin Hood.

Grey and Blue kicked him while he was down. In the ear. In the face. All over his battered body. Brookes could feel a swelling over his left eye. His bottom lip was already engorged with blood, swollen to twice its normal size.

They took an arm each and dragged him to his feet and took it in turns to punch him in his chest again. Blue took the knife and cut a deep gash on his upper arm. Cut the swelling open above his eye. Blood poured down his face. Grey caught him just right with a perfect left hook and splintered his cheek bone. Then threw a massive uppercut and caught Brookes under his chin.

They let go of his arms. Brookes sank to his knees, arms limp by his sides, head bowed. Blue noticed the old scar on his blood-soaked right cheek. He took the knife in his right hand, held Brookes' head up with his left, and reopened the historic wound. Brookes didn't flinch.

Blue took the gun that Brookes had handed him. Sig Sauer P229. Blue pistol-whipped Brookes around the back of his head. He fell sideways and smacked his head on the plinth of Clipsham stone that the statue stands on. Lay prone on the floor. Blue shot him twice. Once in the shoulder, once in the calf. Brookes' body jolted at both shots. Pools of blood appeared from underneath his body.

Satisfied that they had done enough, Blue checked that Brookes was still breathing. He tilted his head slightly to one side to open his airways. He whispered, "Sorry Sir," and he and Grey fled down the hill.

Eleven

The van screeched to a halt behind the other van that Brookes had driven to Nottingham. The team climbed out of the back almost before the vehicle had stopped. Price and Chapman ran towards the side entrance of the station, Roberts carried on along Station Street to the junction with Carrington Street. He stopped on the corner, took his phone out of his pocket.

Kelvin White answered the call. Director Quibell, beads of sweat still present on his head, sat by his side. "Roberts," Kelvin said, no time for banter, not with Quibell in the room.

"Kelvin, can you see me?" Roberts asked as he stood on the corner.

The tech and the Director were staring at the monitor in front of them. Three windows were open. The top left-quarter of the screen showed the CCTV image from the camera on front of the station. Top-right of the screen showed the side view. Bottom-left showed the view from a third camera, across the street, down the pathway to the canal side near the bridge. Bottom-right was blank.

"Yes, we can see you. Thing is, we saw your van turn off Carrington into Station Street, then you disappeared from view as Brookes did. Then you reappeared standing on the corner where you are now. If I were to hazard a guess, I would say the CCTV camera on the side of the station is mounted incorrectly, unless it is intentionally angled to cover the far side of the street. Most of the older models of camera have-"

"So Brookes could have gone that way?" Quibell interjected, impatiently. No time for a CCTV history lesson from White.

"Definitely. If he'd stuck to the inside of the path as Roberts must have done, he'd have been invisible, Sir."

"But you can see me now, Kelvin," Roberts said. "If he did come this way, how did he get across the street without being seen?"

"The camera that we can see you on now is on the front of the station, pivot-mounted. Every forty, forty-five seconds or so it rotates to look in the opposite direction along Carrington."

Even as Kelvin spoke, the camera started moving. Slowly, Roberts disappeared from view. "And… you're gone."

Roberts crossed the street diagonally, down towards the bridge and the pathway by the side of it. He stood at the top of the path, still on Carrington, and asked "What about now, can you see me?" Halfway down the path, Roberts could make out the third camera mounted on the side of the building.

Kelvin looked at the third window, bottom-left of the screen. "No Roberts, nothing."

Roberts moved a little way down the pathway and stood by a four foot high wall on the right-hand side. He peered over and noticed that there was roughly a fifteen foot drop to the canal path. He climbed on to the wall and lowered himself down on the other side, holding on with his fingertips.

"Still can't see you, Roberts," Director Quibell said, checking all of the windows open on the monitor.

Roberts let go of the top of the wall and slid down the side until his feet hit the ground. He bent his knees and rolled over as soon as the contact was made, as a parachutist would do on landing. Got up, dusted himself down. "Right, I'm on the canal path," he replied.

"Never saw a thing," Kelvin said. "If Brookes went that way, that's definitely how he did it."

Director Quibell stood up. "Question is though, Roberts, why? If he did go that way, where was he going?"

"That's what we'll find out, Sir. Kelvin, can you patch me the map of the CCTV blackspots. I'll do a recce of the area."

"On its way now, Roberts," Kelvin replied, always one step ahead.

The line went dead. Director Quibell walked away, then turned back to Kelvin. "Let me know as soon as Roberts or Price get in touch. The PM wants an update. I'll be in my office."

"Sir," Kelvin replied.

Roberts walked along the canal path. There was a footbridge, he recalled, further down, across the canal and towards the city. It was dark, unlit. The moonlight struggled to offer any decent light.

"Roberts, how did it go?" It was Unit Leader Price shouting in his earpiece.

"Made it down to the canal, Sir. Brookes could have come this way and not been since by the cameras. Anything at the station?"

"Negative so far. Few people about. No trains. Checking the waiting rooms and the shops. Jesus, where the hell *is* he?", Price replied. "Keep me informed."

"Will do," Roberts answered.

In the near distance, Roberts could make out the outline of a tall rectangular building, and in front of that, the bridge over the canal. It was just a little too dark to see the two men running over the bridge, coming his way.

Doctor Singh had finished dressing Anna's feet. They were still sore but she felt the pain easing. She slipped her trainers back on cautiously and sat back in her seat. She hated flying, but this was a whole new experience. This was luxury. Right at this moment, Anna felt less nervous about flying than she had ever been at this height. Maybe it was because she couldn't see through the blacked-out windows, her fear of heights not registering. Maybe it was the smoothness and quietness of the Eurocopter's flight. Maybe it was because of her ordeal tonight, that anything after that would seem like a walk in the park. Maybe it was the situation that she found herself in that kept any of the other fears that she would normally have at bay. Maybe it was the constant thoughts in the back of her mind regarding the email which she had read. Maybe the paracetamol that she'd been given weren't paracetamol.

"Ah, excellent," George Butler commented. "It seems we are descending. We'll be there in a few minutes, Miss Farrow."

Doctor Singh double checked that the compartment under his seat was secure then sat back and buckled his seat belt. Anna buckled hers.

"Can't you tell me anything else about what's happening, where we are going?" Anna asked.

George Butler thought for a moment. "You will, I believe, be familiar with conspiracy theories?"

Anna said nothing. She looked at Butler and frowned.

"Tell me about your parents," he said.

"My parents? What has all this got to do with them?" Anna asked, bewildered.

"All this has nothing at all to do with your parents. I was merely intimating that because of the incident surrounding the unfortunate demise of your mother and father, you may have some knowledge of those so-called conspiracy theories."

Confused, Anna thought of her parents, what had happened to them. "They were on holiday. Their dream holiday, they had saved for years and years. Six weeks. A six-week tour of America." Her voice trailed off and her eyes filled with tears. She fell silent for a moment. Remembered. Pictured the photograph of her mother and father that she kept on the chest of drawers in her bedroom. That's how she remembered them. Their smiles. Her mother's arms around her. Her father's sense of humour.

"They were in New York, September 2001," Butler Added, quietly and sympathetically.

Anna nodded. "They were at the World Trade Centre when the planes hit."

"Inside?" Butler asked.

"Outside, just visiting. Taking photos. My father's camera was found..." Anna stared off into the middle distance. Butler gave her a moment. His ears popped as the Eurocopter descended.

"Miss Farrow, I am deeply sorry for your loss. Especially in such circumstances."

"I've never believed the official version of events, Mr. Butler."

Butler nodded. "You don't believe that it was the aeroplanes that caused the twin towers to collapse?"

"Not just that. I don't believe any of the official details."

"It's understandable. You have suffered dreadful grief. Perfectly natural to look for someone or something to blame given the circumstances."

Anna fell silent again. Bowed her head and stared at her hands resting on her lap. Butler felt that he was starting to make some headway, gaining Anna's trust. He tried to keep the conversation going.

"Miss Farrow, there are a hundred conspiracy theories surrounding nine-eleven…"

"And most of them a lot more plausible than the official line!" Anna remarked.

"Such as?"

"Well… sorry, why are we talking about this?"

"It interests me. Please, continue."

"Well, the major sticking point with me is the way the buildings collapsed."

"You think the controlled detonation theory on the twin towers could be true?"

"Absolutely I do. Not just on the towers either. On the World Trade Centre 7 building as well. It always bothered me how those three buildings collapsed so uniformly, and the World Trade Centre 6 building didn't."

Anna was becoming more animated, more passionate. This was a good sign, thought Butler.

"World Trade Centre 6?" he asked.

"Yes. The towers were known as WTC1 and WTC2. WTC1 is the north tower and WTC2 the south tower. According to the official story of events, Mr. Butler, WTC1 was hit first by a plane, shortly followed by another plane hitting WTC2. Now, of course you'll know this, these towers collapsed in on themselves, uniformly, a few hours

127

later. WTC7 collapsed in exactly the same manner some hours after that. The BBC had already reported on the collapse of WTC7 nearly half an hour before it actually did, but that's another anomaly for another day."

Butler smiled at her. She'd certainly done her homework. Poor child, he thought. She'd obviously been distraught at her parents' passing and had spent a great deal of time searching for answers.

"Now, what is not widely talked about," Anna continued, opening up to Butler more and more with each passing moment, "is WTC6. WTC6 stood *directly between* the north tower and WTC7. Yet building 6 did not collapse at all. It was damaged by falling debris, but it did not collapse. And yet, somehow, WTC7, on the opposite side of building 6 from where the planes hit, collapses in exactly the same way as the twin towers."

"Remarkable. What happened to building 6?"

"It had to be demolished shortly after the attacks. A controlled demolition. Ironic. Some of the most senior engineers and architects agree that for the buildings to collapse in the manner in which they did, there had to have been controlled demolitions taking place. A theory backed up by witnesses who actually heard the demolitions in the lower half of every building seconds before the collapse, and video footage widely available online that shows the controlled demolitions actually taking place."

"Well now," Butler said, "that certainly is one conspiracy theory."

"I could go on for hours, Mr. Butler. Don't get me started on the rest. The missile that hit the Pentagon, not a plane, not if you study the hole pattern and the video footage. The flight paths of the planes that hit the twin towers. Would hijacked planes really fly for that long over America and not be challenged by the air force, or was there a stand down order given? The theories are endless and convincing."

"But, of course, they are only conspiracy theories," Butler commented.

"What do you mean?" Anna asked.

"Forgive me, I'm being facetious. A few moments ago, I asked you about conspiracy theories and your familiarity with them. Before we land and you understand more of what is happening, I want to explain the concept of conspiracy theories. You see, the truth of the matter is, I'm afraid, that these theories aren't taken seriously generally, and I'll tell you why. All forms of media, television news, the printed press, online news outlets, when they report on a particular conspiracy theory, it's always done with tongue placed firmly in cheek. Our news outlets, in fact the general media as a whole, make light of these theories in order for them to be seen as untrue and implausible. Why? In order to discredit them. Precisely so the general public see them as just that. Laughable. Incredulous. Unbelievable. To keep the *real* truths from coming out.

"We are told by our governments the version of events that they *want us* to believe, Miss Farrow.

The governments control the media for their own ends. Any theory that possibly debunks their version of events gets made a joke of in the media. Becomes a conspiracy theory. The theory of the controlled demolitions on September the 11th for instance, although backed up by experts in engineering and architecture along with eyewitness accounts, video footage and the laws of physics, is seen as unbelievable because it doesn't 'fit' with the official version of events that the government and the press tells us and needs us to believe. The assassination of JFK for example. Much more plausible that there was more than one shooter on that day in November 1963. The United States government's 'magic bullet' story is incredibly less believable than the theories that have come out since. And yet it's the theories that get laughed off, and the official story that must be true. And it's the way that they are portrayed by the media that causes this reaction.

"It also doesn't help when the wackiest of theories are lumped together with the most plausible. The Royal Family are lizards. The Holocaust never happened. These theories fall under the same umbrella as the completely believable ones. So in the end, Miss Farrow, the term conspiracy theory gets fixed in people's minds as something of a joke. Anything described as a conspiracy theory is therefore laughed at and scorned by the general population, automatically seen as unbelievable by all but the most open-minded person."

"I understand all of that, Mr. Butler. But why are you telling me all this? What has all of this got to do with me?"

George Butler sat back in his seat. "We'll be landing any time now. Then we'll get you the answers you need." His ears popped again with the descent.

Anna thought about Brookes. Hoped he was OK. He had risked his life to protect her, and all the while she had presumed that he was there to harm her. She hoped that she would see him again, to say thank you.

She felt the Eurocopter sway slightly from side to side and she gripped the arms of her seat. Prepared for landing.

Blue and Grey had noticed Roberts coming their way. They had considered their options quickly. Decided that the best course of action was to hide from the agent rather than attack him. If they had confronted him, it probably would have given their positions away. And it wouldn't have been in Brookes' best interest. Best thing for Brookes right now was to be found and hospitalised. They had retreated back to the city side of the footbridge and hidden down the side of one of the bars that overlook the canal.

Roberts was across the footbridge and making his way away from the canal side. He stopped momentarily to check the map on his tablet. He knew that he had to follow the area marked on the map, that was the route that avoided all of the CCTV in the area. It took him along a pathway between two tall buildings and out onto the Canal Street. It was only a short walk to Castle Boulevard. Blue and Grey watched him disappear between the buildings and waited a moment before emerging from their hiding place and moving back towards the footbridge.

Roberts walked along Castle Boulevard checking his map every few steps to make sure he was headed the right way. He had no idea why Brookes would come this way, or if he even did come this way. Had he picked up the target's trail, Roberts wondered. Or was there something else going on. Price and Chapman hadn't checked in, so Roberts was presuming that there was no sign of Brookes or the target at the station.

He stood at the junction of Castle Boulevard and Castle Road and checked his map again. Ahead, along the Boulevard, there were cameras about a hundred yards down. To his right, on Castle Road, there were none. He turned right.

Castle Road climbed gradually up to an old pub, 'Ye Olde Trip to Jerusalem'. Roberts had a quick scout around with his torch and found nothing. The pub looked like it was set into the rock on which the castle stands. On the far side of the pub there was CCTV so Roberts retracked and carried on along Castle Road. To his left, the ancient rock formation gave way to a man-made castle boundary, with pointed-arch doors set into the wall.

132

Roberts made his way along the castle wall boundary. There was a lawned area ahead. The Castle Road came to a dead end, replaced with a wide pedestrianised zone. Roberts spotted some statues a little further up the hill as he shone his torch light around the area. As he approached, he noticed some plaques on the wall. Then his attention was drawn to something slumped on the floor behind the main statue. He directed the torch light at the base as he ran towards it. It was a body. The body of a large male. "Brookes!" he shouted.

Brookes was a mess. His face was completely covered in blood. Deep gashes above his eye and down his cheek. Blood stained legs. His jacket was open, his white vest now soaked in red. He was curled up in the foetal position. He wasn't moving.

Roberts felt for a pulse on the left side of Brookes' neck. Wet with blood, Roberts' fingers pushed against the skin, searching for any sign of life. Nothing.

"Sir. Brookes found!" he said.

"And?" came the immediate response.

"He's been beaten, Sir. Really bad. Trying to find a sign of life."

"Where are you?" Price replied, urgently.

"The castle, by… some statue of Robin Hood."

Chapman's voice was the next one he heard. "I'll get an ambulance," he said, quickly.

Roberts, on his knees in front of Brookes, leant over and put his ear next to Brookes' mouth. Couldn't feel a breath. He tried to find a pulse on

Brookes' wrist and noticed the bullet wound in his shoulder.

"He's been shot, Sir. At least once. And stabbed as well. Can't get a pulse."

"Ambulance on its way. Stay with him. Do all you can to revive him Roberts," Price said.

"Yes Sir," Roberts replied. Afraid to move Brookes in case he did any further damage, Roberts felt that he had no choice. He grabbed the agents' shoulders and hauled him over on to his back. Noticed the huge pools that the body had been lying in, so much blood lost. Tilted his head back and checked the airways were clear. Roberts covered his mouth with his own. Forced his breath into Brookes' limp body. After what seemed like an eternity, Brookes coughed up sticky blood. Roberts recoiled and spat it out, resisting the urge to vomit. Brookes made a wheezing sound and his eyelids fluttered involuntarily.

Twelve

The Eurocopter touched down softly. Doctor Singh and George Butler unfastened their seatbelts. Anna watched as Butler pulled a compact mirror from his trouser pocket and checked his appearance. He smoothed his hair down and adjusted his tie. Made sure his shirt collar was straight. Pulled his waistcoat down to get rid of the creases that had formed as he had been sitting down. Checked the time on his pocket watch, exactly 1.40am. He rechecked his hair. Satisfied with his appearance, he put the mirror away and looked over at Anna. Her hair was dirty and bloodstained, bedraggled and knotty. She had blood and grime all over her face and arms. Her T-shirt was stained and creased. Her leggings and trainers were covered in mud and blood. "Let's get you tidied up, shall we?" he said as Doctor Singh opened the cabin door.

A whoosh of cold night air hit them as they left the Eurocopter cabin. The moonlight seemed brighter, the sky clearer, spattered with stars. Anna noticed that they had landed on a small square of concrete. The Eurocopter was silent, engine off. She could hear the trickle of water straight ahead of her, quite close. She moved toward the sound, leaving the concrete area and walking on short, perfectly trimmed grass down to the water's edge. Doctor Singh motioned to follow her, but Butler put his hand on his shoulder and shook his head, standing back, as if to say *give her a moment*.

As her eyes became adjusted to the darkness, Anna gazed out over the lake. It was a beautiful scene. Moonlight danced and flickered on the water. The silence was all consuming. Ancient trees surrounded the lake on three sides. Under a cascade of branches, two swans were sleeping, heads tucked under their wings, bobbing gently on the water. For a few moments, Anna was lost to the beauty.

George Butler cleared his throat. Anna looked back at him and he smiled at her and held out one arm. "Shall we?" he said quietly. She walked back to the two gentlemen, leaving the lake shore behind. "You will have ample opportunities to visit the lake, Miss Farrow. Right now, we have more pressing matters, but I would also recommend the walk through that wood over there." He pointed to their left to a dense area of mature trees.

The three of them walked back towards the Eurocopter, then walked around the front. The crew were busy in the cockpit, flicking switches and checking buttons. Butler waved at them as they passed and the crew responded with a sharp thumbs up.

Anna was surprised to see the area in front of the Eurocopter. A vast, perfectly manicured lawned area, outlined with trees on the left and right. Ahead, what Anna presumed was the entrance to a huge stately home. It was magnificent and loomed over them as they approached. The façade was lit from the moon that was behind them. Anna could see rows and rows of windows, four stories high in the centre. Huge stone pillars to the left and right. Ancient outbuildings jutting out from both sides, with the appearance of mausoleums or chapels.

As they crossed the lawn, they came to a wide pathway. On the other side, stone steps ten metres wide led up to an upper balcony, and the entrance to the majestic home.

"It's massive," Anna said, breathlessly.

"Impressive, isn't it, Miss Farrow. Nearly eight hundred rooms within. We've been allowed the use of around twenty-five rooms for our offices and other such things. They've been lying empty for centuries. They're in the back wing of course, what was once the servant's quarters. That's why using the rear entrance is so convenient."

Anna stopped and looked up at the grand house in front of her. "This is the rear entrance?" she gasped.

"Quite so," Butler replied.

"Where are we?" Anna asked.

"Hiding in plain sight, Miss Farrow," came the reply.

The ambulance screeched around the corner, turning off Maid Marion Way onto Friar Lane. It made the left onto the pedestrianised area and came to a halt by the statue of Robin Hood. Roberts had stayed with Brookes, checking he was still breathing.

"Ambulance here," he said.

Through his earpiece, Unit Leader Price replied. "Affirmative. En route to Queens Medical Centre. Will meet you there."

The paramedics quickly checked Brookes over and ascertained the extent of his injuries. Rushed for a stretcher. With the help of Roberts they got him into the back of the ambulance. Reversed out of the pedestrian zone and shot off in the direction of the QMC, Nottingham's largest hospital, a little over two miles away.

"Eta three minutes," Roberts said.

"Same." Price replied.

Through the rear entrance, the first room they came to was a vast hall. Wooden floor, stone walls. The ceiling was high above, maybe ten metres, covered with religious paintings. Suits of armour stood along the edges of the hallway. Huge portraits of people Anna didn't recognise hung from the walls, perfectly spaced apart. The biggest crystal chandelier she had ever seen lit the inside space.

Butler wiped his feet on the rug at the doorway. Anna politely followed suit. An elderly, dowdily dressed, woman greeted them, then quickly whispered something in Doctor Singh's ear. He hurried off and disappeared behind a heavy wooden door on the right. Butler looked at the woman. "The Duke. He's had a rough evening, I'm afraid," she said. Butler nodded and looked deep in thought.

"I see." He looked at Anna. "Miss Farrow. This is Mrs. Cranmere. She will see you to your rooms. Please, get freshened up and then we can talk."

My rooms? Anna thought, more confused than ever. "If it's all the same to you Mr. Butler, I would rather just have someone explain to me what is going on. Right now."

Butler acquiesced. "Fair enough. Please, this way. Mrs. Cranmere, please inform the Doctor that we will be in the West Library, should the Duke wish to join us."

Butler walked down the left hallway and Anna followed a few steps behind. Along the wide hall hung more portraits of people long gone. Oil paintings, centuries old, encased in thick gold-plated frames. Earls, Dukes, Barons. There were ornate yet dirty yellow lampshades softening the lighting. Some of the bulbs weren't working. It smelt fusty, dusty, old.

They stopped at an oak double door. Butler went in first. Inside was the complete opposite of how Anna had imagined it. Banks of monitors covered the wall in front of them. In front of the monitors stood a large desk, one chair behind, one in front. A glass conference table stood in the centre of the room, surrounded by eight plush leather office chairs. Along the wall to the left, a water cooler and a coffee machine. A table with a kettle, mugs, sugar, tea bags. A refrigerator underneath the table. To the right, the wall was covered in a huge whiteboard, adorned with scribblings in different coloured marker pens. There were rows of shelves underneath, stacked with books and box files.

The room was air conditioned and the lighting was subtle, not too bright but not dim. Butler moved over to the large desk, Anna following, taking in her surroundings. He sat behind the desk and beckoned Anna to sit opposite. The chair felt comfy as she sat down. Luxurious, like the seat in the Eurocopter.

"Can I get you a cup of tea or coffee, Miss Farrow?" Butler asked.

"No thanks. Just answers," Anna replied.

The ambulance pulled up outside of the main entrance to the Queens Medical Centre. Two porters were waiting at the entrance and they rushed over as Roberts opened the back door. They were wheeling Brookes inside as the black van carrying Price and Chapman pulled up.

"How is he?" Price asked.

"Barely alive," Roberts responded, running behind the porters. They burst through the main entrance, turned right at the main reception desk and ran along the corridor. The porters wheeled Brookes into a waiting open lift. Roberts, Price and Chapman ran past and entered the stairwell.

"Third floor," Roberts shouted to the other two, and they bounded up the stairs, taking them two or three at a time. Roberts reached the third floor corridor and spotted the porters with Brookes a little way down. "This way."

The stretcher crashed through a door into another area, where a doctor was waiting. He held his hand up, stopping the three agents. They watched as Brookes was pushed into a side room, disappearing from view. "No further, gentlemen," the doctor said.

"Government business," Price shouted at the doctor, flashing his ID. "We have to stay with that man."

"Not right now, you don't," the doctor ordered. "He needs emergency surgery. No one goes in except the medical team."

Five or six nurses rushed past them as they stood there.

Roberts looked at Price, who was out of breath.

"Where can we wait?" Chapman asked.

"Right in here," the doctor replied, ushering them into a side waiting room. "I'll update you on the surgery as soon as I have any info."

The doctor left and the door to the waiting room swung shut. They were alone.

Price paced the length of the room twice before anybody spoke. Chapman broke the silence. "What do you reckon?" he said to Roberts.

"He took a hell of a beating," Roberts said. "I thought he was dead. Had to have been a gang. At least two of them." As he spoke he took his phone out of his pocket and pressed speed dial key one. "Hi Kelvin, Roberts again."

Kelvin White had been expecting the call. He had been monitoring the cameras around the area between Nottingham Station and the castle. "What's going on, Andy? What's with the ambulance and our van tearing off to the hospital?"

"We found Brookes. Nearly dead. Must have been attacked by a gang, I reckon. You seen anyone emerge from the area in the last twenty minutes or so?"

"Nope, sorry mate, no-one. Had eyes on all the time."

"Ran the tapes back to see when anyone entered the area?"

"Yep. Nothing out of the ordinary. Just the usual night traffic. Taxis and Buses. Nobody suspicious."

Roberts thought for a moment. Unit Leader Price, clearly agitated, swiped the phone out of his hand. "Kelvin, Price," he barked.

"Sir," Kelvin replied.

"Check again. Someone must have entered and left that area at some point tonight."

"Sir," Roberts interjected, "If no-one was seen coming into or leaving the area, that can only mean one thing."

"I agree. The tech guys have missed something."

"With respect, Sir," Roberts responded, "the tech guys do *not* miss something. If no-one has been picked up leaving the area, they must still be in that area."

"What about actually entering the area though," Chapman asked.

Price looked across at him. "What do you mean?"

"Well Sir, there must be CCTV footage of whoever attacked Brookes entering the area."

"We've covered this," Kelvin said. "No-one suspicious was seen entering the area near the castle. We've gone over the tapes."

"Then whoever attacked Brookes was in the area not covered on CCTV for a long time," Price added. "Whatever, this doesn't add up. We need to talk to Brookes. See why he was there."

"Could be a while before he talks, Sir," Chapman noted. "And it still won't help us in locating the target."

"The target," Roberts thought out loud, "If Brookes was in that area, she must have been in that area as well. Only reason he'd be there. And if Kelvin hasn't seen anyone leave that area, she must still be there."

"That's just about all we have at the moment," Price said. "Kelvin, patch me through to Quibell, Could you?"

"Sir," Kelvin said.

"Better get that IR heli back as well. Sweep the area not covered by the cameras."

"On it," said Roberts.

143

"And you two get back there. Retrace your steps from the castle back to the station. Search everywhere. She must be there somewhere."

"The National Tactical Bureau operates a code hierarchy," George Butler explained. "They categorise their assignment status into either a Code One, a Code Two, or a Code Three." He stood up and cleared his throat. Moved over to the water cooler and removed a plastic cup from the holder. "Want one?" he asked.

Anna sat with her back turned, looking at him. "No thanks," she replied. Feeling chilly, she rubbed her arms to keep warm.

Butler pushed the water lever and filled his cup. He walked back to the desk and noticed Anna shiver. "It is cold in here. I'll ask Mrs. Cranmere to bring you some suitable clothes."

He pressed a button on the phone on the desk. Anna turned to look at the rest of the room. She hadn't noticed when they entered the room that the back wall was covered with another portrait. This time though, she did recognise the figure on the painting. It was a full body, oil on canvas, of Sir Winston Churchill. He was standing against a backdrop of wooden panelling, probably in some ministerial chamber. Stern, round face, an expression that could be mistaken for a frown. Black suit and waistcoat. Spotted bow tie. One hand resting against a leather backed chair, the other raised to waist height, holding a cigar, a thick smoke trail snaking upwards from the tip. It was so well painted that Anna imagined that she could almost smell the tobacco and wood panelling.

Anna turned back as Butler finished the call. "She'll be along presently," Butler remarked. "Now, where was I?"

"Code hierarchies," Anna said.

"Yes, that's right. Now, a Code Three would be something along the lines of... how best to describe it... a leaked document maybe describing an affair or a misdemeanour that may cause embarrassment to a senior government official. Say, for instance, the home secretary was carrying on with his personal secretary. Or the Chancellor had fiddled his tax expenses. That kind of situation. Not earth shattering, but unwanted and potentially damaging to a career."

"There's been a lot of those sort of leaks to the press over the years that I can remember," Anna commented.

"Indeed there has. But you would be amazed how many have been covered up as well, thanks to the NTB. Our members of parliament are not the squeaky-clean bunch of ministers that they would have you believe. Now, a Code Two assignment for the National Tactical Bureau is a different kettle of fish altogether. A Code Two is far more serious. Incredibly damaging. Secret war plans leaked online to our enemies. UK infantry positions, details of routes taken by our armed forces. Base locations. Naval hotspots. Planned air bombing missions. Our defensive weak spots. All leaked online and shared between our most powerful enemies."

Anna shuddered at the thought. So many lives would be lost, families destroyed. The country's security compromised.

"That's a Code Two scenario," Butler continued. "Usually in a Code Two, the NTB works alongside Mi5 or Mi6." He took a sip of water. "You, Miss Farrow, have been classified as a Code One. This is very rare. Hardly ever happens. Whatever has been leaked to you, must be far more serious than any threat to national security. It must be life changing. That's why we are involved. As soon as we heard of a Code One situation at the National Tactical Bureau, the wheels were set in motion. Our priority was the safety and wellbeing of the target. The information acquired is also very important of course."

Anna shuffled uncomfortably in her chair. She knew what she had read on the leaked email and its attachment. Could barely believe it herself, and now she would have to explain it to George Butler and whoever he was involved with. She had kept asking herself where she was and who these people were that had helped her escape from Nottingham. The Doctor, the courier Terri, Butler. Brookes. She hoped Brookes was alright.

There was a heavy rapping at the door, causing Anna to jump. Mrs. Cranmere entered with some blankets.

Price paced the empty waiting room. It had been a brief phone call with Quibell. Not much to report. Target still missing. Brookes incapacitated. Agents searching the most probable area. Quibell sounded resigned to the fact that the target was gone. Could only be a matter of time before the details of the leaked information came out. Quibell signed off quickly, saying he'd been summoned back to the Cabinet Office Briefing Room.

Price was not one for waiting around. He liked to get things done. He paced to the door and swung it open. Walked with purpose down towards the surgery room in which he had seen the porters take Brookes.

Half-way along the corridor, a surgeon emerged from the room. His scrubs were covered in blood splatters. Price slowed up. The surgeon removed his face mask and stood still, staring at the floor. He looked tired, beat. He sensed the presence of the other man and looked up to see Price, dressed exactly the same as the man in the surgery room.

"How is he," Price said.

"You are?" the surgeon asked.

Price flashed his ID again. "That's my man in there."

The surgeon bowed his head. "I'm sorry," he whispered.

"What does that mean?" Price replied, walking towards the surgery room door. He pushed the door but it wouldn't budge. It had an automatic locking device fixed, to keep unauthorised personnel out. "Open this door!" Price demanded.

"Please," the surgeon implored. "There was nothing we could do. His injuries were too severe. Lacerations to his arms and legs. Bullet wounds. Chronic internal bleeding. Punctured lungs. He was dead before he made it to the room."

Price looked through the window in the door. The Doctor he had met previously was standing at the foot of the bed. A nurse turned off the Electrocardiograph machine. Brookes lay lifeless on the bed. His face was a battered mess. The nurse moved slowly around him. Respectfully. She covered his body with a sheet. Placed it over his head. Time of death recorded at 01:56.

"I'm sorry," the surgeon said again.

Price walked slowly over to him. There was an awkward silence.

"Who are you people?" the surgeon asked.

"Do I have your complete confidentiality?" Price murmured, shaken.

"Of course."

"Government agency. This man, he doesn't exist. We don't officially exist."

"We have to inform the next of kin."

"No. He has no next of kin."

"There must be someone."

"There isn't. There's me, and that's it. What will you do with the body?"

"Well, usually we issue a medical certificate and a formal notice..."

"No," Price interrupted. "No certificate, no formal notice."

The surgeon sighed. "The next step is to keep the body in the mortuary here. They will take him down shortly."

"Fine."

The surgeon watched as Price walked away, back towards the stairwell. "We'll be back for the body," he called behind him as he crashed through the door.

Thirteen

George Butler listened to what Anna had to say. She had elicited his complete attention as she'd described the contents of the email and its attachment. He could feel her embarrassment as she recalled every detail, almost as though she couldn't quite believe what she was saying as the words came out.

"Remarkable. Simply remarkable," Butler said. He pushed another button on the phone in front of him and waited for the answer. "Doctor Singh. How is he?"

Anna watched Butler making his phone call.

"He is? Oh, good, good. Would you invite the Duke into the West Library. We have something that he is going to want to hear. Ten minutes? That's fine. We'll be here. Thank you doctor." Butler replaced the handset and sat back in his seat.

They sat in silence for a few moments as the words sank in. Hearing them out loud, Anna felt that they had sounded even more incredulous.

"I can't believe it myself," Anna said, breaking the silence in the room.

"Of course you can't, Miss Farrow. I wouldn't expect you to." He paused. "Do you recall our conversation in the Eurocopter on our way down? The business about conspiracy theories?"

"Yes," she replied.

"About how they are portrayed in the media, the press, how they are ridiculed? It is precisely for that reason that you can't believe. You find the idea ridiculous. And yet, there you saw it, in black and white. They came to kill you for what you've seen. Be in no doubt, this is very real. It has been covered up by the government, and the very topic causes scorn and contempt whenever it's raised."

Anna's head was spinning. It can't be true, yet it *must* be true.

"I want to show you something," Butler continued. He walked over to the shelves underneath the whiteboard. Ran his fingers along the middle shelf until he reached a tatty old box file. Returned to the desk and sat back down opposite Anna.

"Here, take a look at this." He fingered through a pile of paperwork and eventually pulled out a dog-eared black and white photograph. He turned it around and slid it across the desk towards Anna.

The photograph showed a man drawing on a blackboard with chalk. The picture he was drawing showed a diamond shaped object. The dimensions of the diamond were twenty feet across by fourteen feet high.

Butler slid another piece of paper across the desk. A similar drawing, the diamond shaped object, with the same dimensions, this time drawn in pen or pencil. This drawing though had additional details, Anna noted. The words "anti-clockwise rotation" and "hovering five foot off road surface." The drawing was signed.

She looked across the desk at Butler.

"The man in the photo is Alan Godfrey. That's his signature on the sketch. In late November 1980, Alan Godfrey was a police officer with the West Yorkshire Metropolitan Police Force. On patrol, late one evening, near Todmorden, he saw the object he has drawn hovering above the road in front of him. His patrol car stalled and when he tried to call for help, he found his radio wasn't working. His next recollection of events is that he was in a different position, further on up the road, and approximately twenty-five minutes had passed. Another driver along the same stretch of road noticed the same object at the same time. In fact, sightings of the object were reported from as far away as Cliviger, near Burnley, and Halifax."

Anna studied the papers again. Butler continued. "The sketch is the actual drawing taken from Alan Godfrey's police notebook. Mr. Godfrey was highly respected among his peers. He was a police officer, Miss Farrow, with no inclination to manufacture hoaxes and such. This is a true account of what actually happened."

"What happened to him?" Anna asked.

"At first he didn't report the incident for fear of being ridiculed. Then other eye-witness reports of strange lights over the moors surrounding Todmorden came in. He filed an official report. It made national press. The papers reported the incident in their usual tongue-in-cheek manner. Using phrases such as 'Mr. Godfrey *claims…*' and 'Mr. Godfrey *believes…*'. He underwent hypnotic regression, under strict professional conditions, and recounted an abduction. His superiors in the police force tried to have him sectioned. Sections of the media cried hoax. There was no official investigation."

Anna returned the papers back to Butler. He thanked her and placed them back in the box file. Then he pulled out some more papers that were directly underneath.

"As I mentioned, that took place in late November 1980. During that time there were many sightings of these objects reported along the East coast of England and over the North Sea. Just three weeks after Mr. Godfrey's encounter, there was another sighting that sent shockwaves through the government."

Butler passed a photograph to Anna. "This is Lieutenant Colonel Charles Halt, photographed in late 1980, around the time of the incident. Halt was stationed at RAF Bentwaters, in Suffolk, near the

East Anglian coastline. RAF Bentwaters at that time was a United States Air Force base and Halt was Deputy Base Commander.

"It was Boxing Day, around three in the morning. Strange lights were seen outside of the base perimeter at nearby RAF Woodbridge. A security patrol near the East Gate saw lights descend into Rendlesham Forest, close to the base. The patrol, which included Sergeant Jim Penniston, requested permission to leave the base and investigate, thinking it may have been a downed aircraft."

"I think I may have heard about this before," Anna said. "Is this the one they call '*Britain's Roswell*'?"

"Yes it is. Named after the UFO crash in July 1947, seventy-five miles North of Roswell, New Mexico. Now, the patrol entered the forest and reported seeing a metallic object, glowing. As they got closer to it, it moved away through the trees, and the cattle on the farm nearby were described as 'going crazy' in their report. Sergeant Penniston reported that he saw a craft of unknown origin in the forest that night. Later that morning, servicemen from RAF Woodbridge were sent to investigate the forest. They found triangular indentations on the ground, scorch marks and broken branches and abnormal levels of radiation in the area.

"Two days later, Lieutenant Colonel Halt, together with a team of servicemen, returned to the site in Rendlesham Forest. Again, they took radiation samples and recorded higher levels than normal. While they were there, Halt reported seeing three bright lights. One hovered around for three hours and intermittently shot out beams of light.

"Halt wrote a memo to the Ministry of Defence. Subject: Unexplained Lights. He detailed the events of 26th-28th December. I have a copy, here." Butler took another sheet of paper out of the box file and handed it to Anna. She scanned over it. Halt stated in the memo that 'numerous individuals witnessed the activities'. He noted that the object was 'metallic and triangular in shape', that the lights he saw moved 'rapidly in sharp angular movements' and were 'red, green and blue'.

"The Ministry of Defence stated that the event posed no threat to national security, and never investigated further. It was covered up, Miss Farrow, just like the Alan Godfrey incident. Shocking to think that two major incidents like this happened just three weeks apart."

"Why would the MoD not, at least, investigate?"

"Why indeed? Here we have a Sergeant and a Lieutenant Colonel in the US Air Force, and well respected servicemen, reporting unidentified objects near an army base. There is only one explanation as to why the MoD didn't investigate. Because they already knew what they would find. They know what these unidentified craft are. Sceptics have tried to debunk the incident over the years. It was the light from a lighthouse. It was merely atmospheric lighting effects. Shooting stars. Static stars.

Muntjac deer. A security policeman, driving with modified lights on his car. The supposed explanations change more often than the wind, yet none of them come close to what the Sergeant and the Deputy Base Commander saw. There was even a laughable attempt to explain the events away as recently as 2018. This latest explanation is that it was the Special Air Service! The SAS had staged a hoax on RAF Woodbridge. Because the SAS of course, they don't have anything better to do. Incredible."

Anna Farrow sat wide-eyed at the desk, her hands resting on her lap, a blanket covering her shoulders. "I think I'd like that glass of water now," she whispered.

Butler replaced the Halt papers back into the box file and pulled out a tatty Ordnance Survey map. He stood up and walked over to the large glass conference table. Spread the huge map out. "I'll put the kettle on, Miss Farrow," he said. "The Duke will want his cup of tea when he arrives."

Cabinet Office Briefing Room A was buzzing with activity. The Prime Minister sat in his chair, to his left sat the Chief of the Defence Staff and to his right the Vice-Chief. The Director General of Mi5 and the Head of Mi6 were either end of the line-up. The Chief of the Air Staff sat on the opposite side of the table with the Commander Strategic Command. Sandwiched between, Director Quibell of the National Tactical Bureau, looking solemn. Behind

157

them, their secretaries and personal assistants milled about, talking on phones, waving pieces of paper in the air.

"Gentlemen," Quibell said above the general noise, "the situation has worsened. The target is still missing, although we have a good idea of the area in which she may be hiding. One of our agents, I have been informed, was attacked and taken to the Queens Medical Centre in Nottingham a short while ago. Unfortunately, his injuries were too serious, and he has died as a result."

The room hushed and fell silent for a moment. The Prime Minister broke the silence. "Who was he?"

"Joseph Brookes, Prime Minister. One of our best. We can't say exactly what happened, how he sustained his injuries, but we believe it must have been a gang who attacked him. We are confident that they are still in the area and they will be found and dealt swift justice."

"Find them," the Prime Minister said coldly. "Found out why they attacked the agent."

"We will," Quibell said confidently.

"And the Farrow woman? You say you know where she may be?"

"There is an area close to the castle in Nottingham that appears to be out of range of any Close Circuit Cameras. That area was where Brookes was found after he had been attacked. We are assuming that he was following her at the time of the attack. We are monitoring every camera on the periphery of the area in question. Nobody has been seen exiting the area. So our feeling is she's still there somewhere. Agents are there now. We have a chopper with thermal and infra-red imaging up in the air. If she's there, we'll find her."

"Yes, I seem to recall you saying something similar on the last occasion we were in this room, Director."

Quibell said nothing. The Chief of the Defence Staff spoke next. "Has there been any leak from the target that we know of as yet?"

"No, Sir," Quibell replied. "She has no way of contacting anyone. No access to internet. The details of the email are known only to her."

"But we have to presume the worst, Director," The Vice-Chief commented. "We have to come up with a plausible explanation for the information contained in the leaked document."

"Correct," the Prime Minister said, "Just in case the target isn't found, and the information does become public knowledge. That is why we are here."

The door to COBRA opened and in walked a smartly dressed woman. Quibell looked over at her and rolled his eyes. The Head of the Ministry of Defence.

"Sorry I'm late gentlemen," she said as she walked around the table and sat down next to the head of Mi6. "Something important at the office." She placed a file of papers on the table.

"More important than this?" the Prime Minister huffed. "I don't need to remind you that it's your department that caused this mess."

Quibell smiled inwardly.

Anna Farrows straightened her skirt under her and blushed slightly. "Prime Minister, I would like to sincerely apologise again for the actions of my office. I asked a colleague to send a copy of the new plans to my personal email address for me to work on remotely. I realise the seriousness of the mistakes made and take full responsibility."

"We can deal with that matter once we have fixed this current situation," the Prime Minister responded. "Can we have the room cleared please."

The secretaries and personal assistants walked to the exit and left, leaving the seated dignitaries alone in the briefing room. One by one they turned to look at Director Quibell.

"You too," said the Prime Minister. "You have an assignment to head. We wouldn't want you to be side-tracked by what we have to discuss. Keep me informed of any progress."

Director Quibell looked at each one in turn. Then stood up and walked towards the exit.

"Find that woman, Director. Make this meeting we're about to have a complete waste of our time."

Quibell nodded and left the room. The door closed behind him. He loosened his tie and undid the top button of his shirt. Made his way back to the National Tactical Bureau.

Fourteen

The doors to the West Library opened and Doctor Singh entered. He kept the doors open for the man behind.

George Butler greeted him. "Doctor Singh. Any news on Agent Brookes?"

Butler and Anna had moved to the glass conference table. They were sitting next to each other, on the left side near the drinks table. Butler had been explaining to Anna the pen markings drawn on the Ordnance Survey map of the British Isles.

Doctor Singh joined them and stood behind them. "He's at Queens Medical Centre. I'll know more shortly. I'm in contact with the Medical Director."

Anna kept her eyes on the open double doors.

The Duke appeared.

Anna inhaled sharply, her eyes-widened, stunned. *Is that who I think it is?* Instinctively she stood up straight. Butler stayed in his seat. She panicked. She didn't know how to curtsey. She half-heartedly tried her best. The Duke, watching her, raised his eyebrows. "Is that the best you've got, girl?" he said. His voice was faint and croaky.

Anna blushed. She looked away, she was sure she had read somewhere that you shouldn't make eye contact. She looked down at Butler. He smiled back at her. She threw him a confused glance.

The Duke laughed, a glint in his eye. "Please Miss, sit down will you. I've had a bloody lifetime of being bowed to and whatnot. If I can talk frankly in front of you, I've had bloody enough of it. We don't stand on ceremony here. We leave all of that pomp and nonsense for the outside."

The Duke closed the doors behind him and shuffled over to the glass table. He walked slowly with the aid of two sticks. He made it to the chair opposite Anna. Doctor Singh walked around the table to help him.

"Don't you bloody dare, doctor," the Duke called out. "I know how to sit down without aid."

"Sir," the doctor replied, and retreated behind Butler.

The Duke sat down and propped his sticks up against the adjacent seat. Cleared his throat and rested his old hands on top of the map in front of him. He looked across the table at Anna. "Dear, that was possibly the most awful curtsey I have ever had the pleasure to endure."

She blushed again.

Butler laughed. "He's teasing you, Miss Farrow. Take no notice of the Duke when he's in this mood."

"You know me too well," the Duke replied. "You've been with me for too long, Butler. Far too long."

"Twenty-five laborious years, Sir."

The Duke laughed then looked back at Anna and studied her for a moment. "So. You're the tolling bell."

Anna frowned, confused at the Duke's remark. "I'm Sorry Sir, the tolling bell?"

Butler responded. "No tolling bell. That's the Duke's nickname for the National Tactical Bureau. NTB."

"You're the tolling bell, dear," the Duke added. "The National Tactical Bureau don't want you to toll, to talk. Their aim is to silence you, to make sure that you do not divulge what you have learned. To make sure that there is… no tolling bell."

"I see," Anna replied. "Then yes. I am that, Sir."

The doctor noticed a cup of tea on the side table. He picked it up and handed it to Butler, who passed it over to the Duke. He sipped it and grimaced. "No sugar, Butler."

"No Sir, you are not allowed it. Isn't that right, doctor?"

"Yes, that is right," Doctor Singh replied.

"I don't bloody care what's allowed and what's not. Stick three sugars in there would you?" he said, passing the cup back to Anna. "I can't drink tea without sugar. And I'll take three, for no other reason than to try and keep myself awake whilst in your company, Butler."

163

Butler shook his head. The doctor sighed. Anna sorted the sugars and passed it back to the Duke. He tasted it. "That's better, thank you."

"You're welcome, Sir," Anna replied and smiled sweetly.

"Well now, young tolling bell. It's been a long night and you must be tired. You'll stay here as our guest for as long as you like. We have a spare suite or thirty in this wing. Tomorrow you'll meet the rest of this little team of Butler's."

"Thank you, Sir," Anna said. "Can I ask what it is that you do here?"

"Butler will fill you in with all those details. First, you must tell me what it is that you have inadvertently learned this evening."

Anna fell silent. She looked at Butler. "Tell him what you told me, Miss Farrow."

Anna took a deep breath. She hoped it wouldn't sound as crazy as it had sounded when she had told Butler.

"Well Sir. Yesterday evening I read an email that wasn't meant for me. It was addressed to an Anna Farrows, Head of the Ministry of Defence. It described a secret air base. Underneath a reservoir, called Wishaw-Dean or something like that."

Butler interjected. "We've checked the map. Miss Farrow was unsure of the specific name. There is a Walshaw Dean reservoir. Three actually. Right on the Pennine Way, in the middle of nowhere. North of Todmorden and Hebden Bridge, on the moors. Very remote. The three Walshaw Dean

164

reservoirs are all connected. See here," he said and pointed to an area of the map laid out in front of them on the table. Three small blue blobs, the Pennine Way dotted running next to them, and nothing else for miles. No roads, no landmarks.

"An underground air base. You realise how crazy that sounds?" the Duke commented. "An *underground* air base."

Anna's heart sank. Not the reaction from the Duke she had wanted.

"Not an air base for our Forces Sir. For storing... otherworldly craft."

The Duke leant forward. "Extra-terrestrial craft?"

"Yes Sir," Butler beamed.

Anna shuddered. It still sounded irrational, even though she had seen the email with her own eyes. Even after Butler had educated her about the incidents back in 1980 and showed her on the map all of the locations marked in pen, where the hundreds of eye-witness reports had confirmed sightings of unexplained craft. All covered up by the MoD. All ridiculed in the press. It's no surprise that only a small minority of people believe, she knew that now. She had seen enough evidence tonight to silence even the hardest of sceptics.

"Miss Farrow, please continue," Butler said.

"Well Sir, that's not all. There is another one. Another underground base, I mean. Underneath Thetford Forest in Norfolk. And the two bases are linked by an underground tunnel."

The Duke sat back in his chair, deep in thought.

Butler pointed to the map on the table. "If you draw a straight line from the Walshaw Dean reservoirs to Thetford Forest, shown here, that's about a distance of two hundred miles. All of the major sightings from 1980 onwards happen around where the line passes through or to the East of that line. The Ministry of Defence have underground bases harbouring alien craft and who knows what else, and the bases are linked by one long tunnel."

The Duke struggled to his feet, grabbing his sticks as he rose. Anna watched as he limped over and stood in front of the huge portrait on the wall near the double doors. He looked up into the painted eyes of the man before him and smiled.

"You old dog," he said to the painting. "You bloody old bulldog! Wipe that frown off your face man. Smile for once."

Anna turned to Butler. He smiled and shook his head. "The Duke and Churchill had a shared interest in unidentified flying objects. An obsession for both of them, some might say. They both became fascinated by the subject during the Second World War. Spent many an afternoon discussing the topic over a bottle of whisky."

The Duke turned around. "Towards the end of the war, one of our RAF reconnaissance planes was returning home. Over the English Channel it was followed by an unidentified craft, which flew alongside it for a while before accelerating at great speed and disappearing at an impossible angle.

166

Winnie got to hear of it and became obsessed. He immediately ordered a cover up. Said it could cause great panic in the population and could destroy belief in the church."

"There were a lot of sightings during the latter days of World War 2," Butler added. "Foo fighters, the Americans and allied troops called them. Unexplained phenomena. Strange lights in the sky, weirdly shaped metallic objects. They buzzed our aircraft, flew around them, followed them, before turning at impossible angles, darting left and right, flying off at great speed. Our greatest military minds investigated them, such was the concern. It was thought that they could possibly be enemy weapons, with vastly superior technology than what was available to our side."

"Could it not have been?" Anna asked.

"Those particular fears were soon laid to rest. British Intelligence learned that the enemy shared the same concerns. Japanese and German airmen were reporting similar experiences. The other side thought *we* were responsible. But if it wasn't *us* and it wasn't *them*..." Butler trailed off, letting the words hang in the air.

The Duke slowly walked back to the table. "Winnie met with US General Dwight Eisenhower. They talked at great length about the foo fighters. Decided the best course of action would be a complete cover up of the events. On this side of the pond, the Ministry of Defence were charged with coordinating the cover up, and they have been in charge of it ever since."

The Duke sat back down and had a sip of his tea. "The subject fascinates me dear," he said to Anna. "Always has."

"Miss Farrow," Butler said, "As explained a little while ago, you are a National Tactical Bureau Code One. It is very rare for there to be a Code One. What you have told us so far tonight could cause devastating shockwaves throughout this country and around the world."

"So far?" the Duke butted in. "Is there more?"

"Yes, there's more Sir," Butler remarked. "Miss Farrow has also seen part of a highly classified document detailing reverse engineering. Taking the technology from extra-terrestrial craft, breaking it down, learning from it. The information is shared between the MoD and Area 51 in Nevada, where similar engineering takes place. It's all true Sir. If this was widely known, think of the implications."

The Duke looked across at Anna, who nodded in agreement. "I only saw a little of that document, but that seemed to be the essence of it. It detailed how to travel at great speed without the need for fuel. They use the tunnel between the two bases as a sort of test track. I was reading this part when the email deleted. The last thing I read was that they had managed to travel between the two bases in a matter of seconds."

"Two hundred miles in a matter of seconds," The Duke gasped. He looked down at the map on the table.   Studied the line Butler had drawn from Thetford Forest to the Walshaw Dean reservoirs. "Incredible."

"Incredible that a tunnel has actually been built all that way underground," Anna remarked.

"Hmm? No, that part is easy," Butler said. "Take the London Underground. 250 miles of tunnel network, some built 50 metres below the capital. The tunnels are vast. The platforms, the walkways, the escalators. All deep underground. Built under the Thames. We were capable of that decades ago. Parts of the London underground are over 150 years old.   Built in the Victorian Age, Miss Farrow. Without today's technology and capabilities."

"Built with the blood, sweat and tears of incredible men, to quote old Winnie," the Duke remarked.

Anna hadn't thought of it in that way. She remembered trips to London with her parents when she was young. Being so excited at travelling on the tube, riding the big escalators deep down underground. The darkness as the train clicked and clacked between stations. The hustle and bustle. The wind on the platforms. It now seemed to her that another underground tunnel linking Norfolk to the North was perfectly plausible.   Anna's mind wandered to the tunnels underneath Nottingham and the castle.   Crude by today's standards, but impressive none the less. Built centuries ago, miles of secret subterranean passageways and caves. She

169

thought about her escape through that dark tunnel network. She thought about Brookes.

The Duke interrupted her thoughts. "Thank God for the ineptitude of the Ministry of Defence. Without that, we wouldn't know all of this," he laughed. Butler and the doctor smiled.

"The Duke and the MoD don't get on," Butler said to Anna. "The MoD have to categorically deny any existence of extra-terrestrial activity, even though they currently have operatives working on a UFO project. The project was set up in 1952 by Churchill and carries on to this day. Churchill and the Duke were great friends, and they would discuss the matter in great detail until Churchill's death back in '65. What irks the Duke so much is that the Ministry of Defence are servants of the Crown, and as such should be answerable to him. That they lie to him on this subject and deny their obvious involvement causes animosity. That is why the Duke has organised our little set-up here."

"I simply want to get to the truth, you see," the Duke added. "And I never thought I would live to hear that truth. Thank you, Miss Farrow."

There was silence in the room. The Duke looked tired. The doctor looked concerned. "Sir, you should get some rest now."

"Yes, thank you doctor, I believe I should. We will talk more in the morning Miss Farrow. Please rest well."

Anna stood up as the Duke rose. "Thank you, Sir. And you."

The doctor followed the Duke as they left the room. He closed the doors behind him and Anna sat back down, next to Butler.

"You should try and rest as well, Miss Farrow. Tomorrow we will talk more. I'll show you around, give you the grand tour."

"I don't think I'll sleep tonight Mr. Butler." Anna replied.

"No, I wouldn't be surprised if you didn't."

"I can't go home, can I?"

"No, I'm afraid you can't. Not for a long time. Too dangerous."

Anna stood up and looked at the map on the table. She looked at Nottingham and thought of her little house. Then her eyes followed the road network down to the South-West of the country.

"My brother, Ian, and his family. Will they be OK?"

"Your family will be fine. They will be informed of what has happened. We'll work something out. They are in no danger."

"Thank you, Mr. Butler."

"Let me finish up here, tidy this lot away, then I'll show you to your suite."

Fifteen

The mortuary at the Queens Medical Centre is located at the rear of the main building on the ground floor. Brookes' body lay on a trolley in the centre of the room, covered by a sheet. The doctor and the nurse stayed with the body after the porters had left.

The room was rectangular, white and bright. White floors, white ceiling. Rows of floor to ceiling metallic fridges along the longer sides. At the far end, a set of double doors led to a loading bay. There was a tray on a trolley at one side of the room, containing autopsy instruments. Scalpel, rib shears, saw, chisel, hammer, forceps, skull elevator, scissors.

The mortician was absent. He wasn't needed for what was to come.

The nurse removed her cap. Shook her hair loose. The doctor watched her. Said nothing. She walked over to where Brookes lay. Lifted the sheet and uncovered his head.

"How are you feeling?" she asked.

Brookes wheezed and coughed. "Felt better," he said faintly.

"Try not to say too much, you're in bad shape."

"What's happening Terri," he murmured.

"Shhh. Don't speak. Change of plan. You're dead."

Brookes opened one eye, the other being too swollen. "Dead? Not sure I like that plan." A pain in his chest made him groan.

Terri chuckled. "Got a call from Doctor Singh. He asked his contacts here to fake your death. To say you were too wounded to save."

"Why?"

"Not entirely sure, there hasn't been a lot of time for explanations. When I spoke to him, he briefly mentioned that you were no longer needed inside the NTB, he said that they had another person in mind to fill your boots inside there. I don't know who, but I suppose we will find out."

"So I just work for the Duke now." Brookes croaked. He wondered who the new mole would be in the National Tactical Bureau. Then he stopped wondering. It hurt his head too much.

"Doctor Singh asked me to drive you back. He'll fix you up."

The doctor, waiting patiently, stood forward. "Mr. Brookes, you have sustained serious injuries tonight. But I'm pleased to say that none of them are life threatening. We have patched you up the best we can, given the short time scale. I can give you something for the pain for your journey."

"No, thanks anyway," Brookes whispered.

"We should get going. Doctor, would you mind?" Terri said, motioning towards the loading bay exit.

The doctor rushed to the rear of the room and opened the double doors. Backed up just outside, with the rear doors wide open and a ramp leading up inside, an ambulance. A driver waited in the front cab. Terri pushed the trolley up into the rear. Secured it in place. Strapped Brookes down as softly but securely as she could. Sat next to him.

"Give Doctor Singh my regards," the doctor shouted, standing by the rear doors, as the engine started.

"Will do," Terri replied.

The doctor slammed the ambulance doors shut and gave the driver a thumbs-up in his wing mirror. The driver stuck his hand out of the open window and waved in reply. Pulled away slowly.

Brookes opened his one good eye and turned his head to look over at Terri. "The Target?" he asked, quietly.

"Safe," Terri replied.

"Good," said Brookes. He turned his head back and closed his eye.

Butler walked Anna to her suite along the dusty hallways. A stark contrast to the West Library in which she had met the Duke. She was still reeling from the shock of it all.

A large Grandfather Clock showed her it was just after two-thirty in the morning. Three hours ago, she thought to herself, she had been lying in her own bed, unable to sleep. Staring at the soft green digits on her bedside alarm clock, head spinning.

"Not much further now," Butler remarked as they walked on. The hallways were long and wide. The floor was carpeted a light beige colour but was wearing thin through decades of wear and tear. The walls were covered in walnut panelling, layers of dust on the panel frames. The lighting was dim, wall mounted lamps covered with tatty shades, some not working.

"As you can probably tell," Butler said, "this wing doesn't get used much these days. But I am sure you will be more than comfortable here."

Anna nodded. "It's all a bit overwhelming at the moment, Mr. Butler. A lot to take in."

"I'm sure it is, Miss Farrow."

They stopped at a large wooden door. "Ah, here we are. This is your suite. Will there be anything else? Would you like me to send for a nightcap or glass of water for you?"

Anna shook her head and smiled. "Thank you, but no."

"Very well. Good night, Miss Farrow. Sleep well. I'll be along in the morning with breakfast." Butler turned to leave.

Anna opened the door to her suite, then paused.

"Mr. Butler?" she cried out.

"Yes?", he replied as he turned round.

"I was just wondering, what will you do with the information you now have?"

"We will sit down tomorrow with the Duke, go through it in more detail. There is much work to be done."

Butler paused for a moment in case Anna had any further questions. She hadn't.

"Until tomorrow then, Miss Farrow."

"Good night," she said, and entered her suite.

Anna closed the door behind her and noticed there was a key in the lock. She looked around the room. It felt huge. High ceiling with an ornate chandelier throwing a soft, warm light. The bed was a super king-size at least, she thought. The bedside tables were old-fashioned. There was a phone on one of them. The carpet was thick and plush. The curtains were open, floor to ceiling, and Anna noticed a two-seater settee positioned in the large bay window. There was an old table with tea and coffee making facilities in the far corner. On the adjacent wall there were two doors off to the right.

She locked the door behind her. Her paranoia had not yet gone completely. She kicked off her trainers and felt the luxurious carpet between her toes.

Anna walked over to the first door and entered the next room. There was a free-standing bath in the centre and a separate shower off to one corner. A mirror covered the back wall. Three thick towels hung over the wall mounted radiator. Another inner door led to a toilet and sink.

Anna walked back to the bedroom and across the room to the second door. This opened out into a large living area. There was a huge three-piece suite and a television on the wall. It was a very comfortable looking room, airy and warm. Shelves of books stood either side of a modest open fireplace. Another door off to the right led to yet another room. This had been set up as a study. It had a desk with a laptop, an office chair and more bookshelves crammed full of reading material.

Back in the bedroom, Anna sat on the bed. Bounced a couple of times to check how hard it was. She noticed a pile of clothes, neatly folded, near the pillows. Nightwear. A selection for her to choose from.

She walked over to the bay window and slumped down on the settee. There was a blanket hanging over the back. She pulled it and wrapped it around her and snuggled into the cushions. Anna lay her head on the settee arm and gazed out of the window, onto the gardens of Buckingham Palace.

There was a beautiful full moon. It lit up the perfectly manicured lawns beyond the balcony area outside the window. It was so bright, Anna could just make out the swans far off in the distance, asleep on the lake.

Authors Note

WARNING: SPOILERS

This book is a work of fiction and, except in the case of historical fact as noted below, any similarity to actual persons, living or dead, is purely coincidental.

The incidents as described in chapter thirteen of this book, concerning the details of the encounters in November and December 1980, are well documented. The events have been retold here as accurately as possible, only minor embellishments have been made for the sake of narrative.

Declassified documents released to the National Archives suggest that Sir Winston Churchill ordered a cover up of a ufo sighting during World War 2, as recounted in chapter fourteen of this book. The meeting with General Eisenhower and the subsequent joint cover up is also well documented online.

Other documents released confirm that, in the 1950's, there was a 'Flying Saucer Working Party' (FSWP), set up by the Ministry of Defence. On the

28th July 1952, Churchill wrote a memo to the Secretary of State for Air, Lord Cherwell, outlining his concern and asking for a report into 'flying saucers'.

On average, in the United Kingdom, a sighting of an unidentified flying object has been officially reported every day since the turn of the millennium. In the United States, a sighting is officially reported once every hour, on average.

Official figures state that 95% of these sightings can be explained. The other 5% remain unsolved.

Jon Marks
April 2020

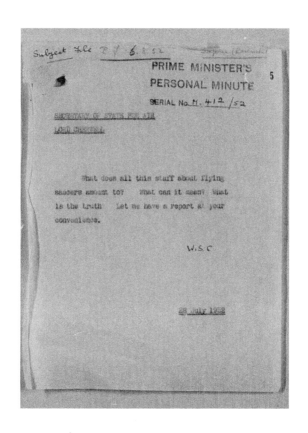

PRIME MINISTER'S
PERSONAL MINUTE 5

SERIAL No. M. 412 /52

SECRETARY OF STATE FOR AIR

LORD CHERWELL

What does all this stuff about flying
saucers amount to? What can it mean? What
is the truth? Let me have a report at your
convenience.

W.S.C

28 July 1952

Sir Winston Churchill's minute to Lord Cherwell,
28th July 1952.

Image: National Archives PREM 11/855

Contains public sector information licensed under the Open
Government Licence v3.0

183

RAF LIAISON OFFICE
Royal Air Force Bentwaters Woodbridge Suffolk IP12 2RQ

Telephone Woodbridge 3737 ext ~~2233~~ 2257

MOD (DS8a)

Your reference

Our reference BENT/019/76/
AIR

Date *15* January 1981

UNIDENTIFIED FLYING OBJECTS (UFO's)

I attach a copy of a report I have received from
the Deputy Base Commander at RAF Bentwaters concerning some mysterious sightings in the Rendlesham forest near RAF Woodbridge. The report is
forwarded for your information and action as considered necessary.

D H MORELAND
Squadron Leader
RAF Commander

Copy to:

SRAFLO, RAF Mildenhall

Covering letter for the Halt report sent to the
Ministry of Defence, 15th January 1981.

DEPARTMENT OF THE AIR FORCE
HEADQUARTERS 81ST COMBAT SUPPORT GROUP (USAFE)
APO NEW YORK 09755

REPLY TO
ATTN OF.   CD

13 Jan 81

SUBJECT: Unexplained Lights

TO: RAF/CC

1. Early in the morning of 27 Dec 80 (approximately 0300L), two USAF
security police patrolmen saw unusual lights outside the back gate at
RAF Woodbridge. Thinking an aircraft might have crashed or been forced
down, they called for permission to go outside the gate to investigate.
The on-duty flight chief responded and allowed three patrolmen to pro-
ceed on foot. The individuals reported seeing a strange glowing object
in the forest. The object was described as being metalic in appearance
and triangular in shape, approximately two to three meters across the
base and approximately two meters high. It illuminated the entire forest
with a white light. The object itself had a pulsing red light on top and
a bank(s) of blue lights underneath. The object was hovering or on legs.
As the patrolmen approached the object, it maneuvered through the trees
and disappeared. At this time the animals on a nearby farm went into a
frenzy. The object was briefly sighted approximately an hour later near
the back gate.

2. The next day, three depressions 1 1/2" deep and 7" in diameter were
found where the object had been sighted on the ground. The following
night (29 Dec 80) the area was checked for radiation. Beta/gamma readings
of 0.1 milliroentgens were recorded with peak readings in the three depressions and near the center of the triangle formed by the depressions.
A nearby tree had moderate (.05-.07) readings on the side of the tree
toward the depressions.

3. Later in the night a red sun-like light was seen through the trees.
It moved about and pulsed. At one point it appeared to throw off glowing
particles and then broke into five separate white objects and then disappeared. Immediately thereafter, three star-like objects were noticed
in the sky, two objects to the north and one to the south, all of which
were about 10° off the horizon. The objects moved rapidly in sharp angular
movements and displayed red, green and blue lights. The objects to the
north appeared to be elliptical through an 8-12 power lens. They then
turned to full circles. The objects to the north remained in the sky for
an hour or more. The object to the south was visible for two or three
hours and beamed down a stream of light from time to time. Numerous individuals, including the undersigned, witnessed the activities in paragraphs
2 and 3.

CHARLES I. HALT, Lt Col, USAF
Deputy Base Commander

The Halt report, 13th January 1981.

Image: Public Domain Mark 1.0

Loose Minute

DR/3/7/8

27 September 1999

Sec(AS)2

ENQUIRY FROM A MEMBER OF THE PUBLIC: Section 40

1. You would wish to be aware of this transfer from HQ Sy to Defence Records. Find attached copies of a number of papers received by HQ Sy from **Section 40** on the subject of a strange occurrence that occurred in the early 1940s that was subsequently the subject of a discussion between Churchill and Eisenhower.

2. Churchill's interest in the subject are contained in a file preserved in the Public Record Office under reference *PREM 11/855*, dating from 1952 he asked for a report on "flying saucers". In reply the SofS Air dismissed stories about flying stories. It may be the case that Mr Churchill expressed an earlier interest, but this would be a matter for No 10/Cabinet Office.

3. So far as the MOD is concerned we know of no closed records dating from World War II on this subject.

4. It may be the case that you would wish to reply to **Section 40** If not, I propose respond robustly, advising that we are unaware of any closed defence records on this subject dating from the time of WWII and referring him to the PRO and Cabinet Office (assuming he wishes to pursue his research).

MINISTRY OF DEFENCE
SEC (AS) 2
2 8 SEP 1999
FILE

Internal correspondence regarding the Churchill/Eisenhower meeting on UFO's, dated 27th September 1999

Image: National Archives DEFE 24/2013/1

Contains public sector information licensed under the Open Government Licence v3.0

Your Reference: D/HQ Sy 1/107/8/3
My Reference: MOD_3
Date: 20 September 1999

Re: Information reported to myself concerning the incident.

A report from an RAF aircrew approaching the east coast of England after a mission into Germany sometime in the early 1940's was discussed by leaders in the UK and the US.

The aircraft was intercepted by an object of unknown origin, which matched course and speed with the aircraft for a time and then underwent an extremely rapid acceleration away from the aircraft probably with non-ballistic or non-aerodynamic flight characteristics. Photographs and/or film was obtained by this aircrew showing a metallic arrow-shaped body. This event was discussed by Mr Churchill and General Eisenhower, neither of whom knew what had been observed. There was a general inability for either side to match a plausible account to these observations, and this caused a high degree of concern.

Section 40 was not present during the initial discussion when this event was communicated to the US but he was present at the follow-up meeting when the response from the US was received. He made up his own mind (privately) that no technological capability was known at that time which could account for the observed event. Several years later he felt that this event was of sufficient importance to communicate to another person in a minimum-risk way despite the restrictions imposed by the Official Secrets Act.

1. The RAF aircraft involved was a reconnaissance plane returning to England from a photographic mission to either France or Germany during the latter part of the War.
2. The encounter with the unknown object occurred close to or over the English coastline.
3. The observed object was undetected until it was close to the aircraft. It was suddenly observed by the aircrew appearing at the side of the aircraft at a very high speed; then it very rapidly matched its speed with that of the aircraft.
4. It appeared to "hover" noiselessly relative to the aircraft for a time. One of the photographic airmen began to take photographs of it. It appeared metallic but its shape was not described. (Please disregard my earlier comment about an "arrow-shaped" body, this appears to have been an error on my part).
5. The object very suddenly disappeared, leaving no trace of its earlier presence.
6. During the discussion with Mr. Churchill, a consultant (who worked in the Cumbria area during the War) dismissed any possibility that the object had been a missile, since a missile could not suddenly match its speed with a slower aircraft and then accelerate again. He declared that the event was totally beyond any imagined capabilities of the time. Another person at the meeting raised the possibility of an unidentified flying object, at which point Mr. Churchill declared that the incident should be immediately classified for at least 50 years and its status reviewed by a future Prime Minister. . . . . with a former airman who possessed some

Excerpts from correspondence sent to Ministry of Defence, September 1999. Name of author remains classified

Images: National Archives DEFE 24/2013/1

For all the latest information on forthcoming releases, visit:

Jon Marks Author on Facebook

Jonmarksauthor on Instagram

@MarksAuthor on Twitter

Printed in Great Britain
by Amazon